THUNDER AT
RIVER STATION

To Frank Pecorich
and Pam

With my best wishes
to you and your wife.
It's been a pleasure for
our opportunity of meeting.

Enjoy,

Stan Briney

THUNDER AT
RIVER STATION

STAN BRINEY

TATE PUBLISHING
AND ENTERPRISES, LLC

Published by Tate Publishing & Enterprises, LLC
127 E. Trade Center Terrace | Mustang, Oklahoma 73064 USA
1.888.361.9473 | www.tatepublishing.com

Tate Publishing is committed to excellence in the publishing industry. The company reflects the philosophy established by the founders, based on Psalm 68:11,
"The Lord gave the word and great was the company of those who published it."

Book design copyright © 2015 by Tate Publishing, LLC. All rights reserved.
Cover design by Junriel Boquecosa
Interior design by Manolito Bastasa

Published in the United States of America

ISBN: 978-1-63367-409-7
1. Fiction / Westerns
2. Fiction / Historical
14.11.03

I want to dedicate this novel to my five adult grandchildren—Garrett, Cassidy, Grant, Carlye, and Grayson. Each one of these wonderful young people has provided me with untold great joy, pride, and love. I applaud their character and their many outstanding achievements.

ACKNOWLEDGEMENTS

The successful publication of any prose requires the work of many individuals assisting the author along the way. I owe a deep sense of gratitude to everyone who has made this book possible.

First and foremost, I must express my thanks and deepest appreciation to my wife, Priscilla, for her patience, understanding, and encouragement while I toiled untold hours on the research and subsequent writing of the initial manuscript.

My friend and a very successful author in his own right, Sam Dawson provided considerable technical knowledge and assistance at times when I needed it most.

My sketches received the expertise and painstaking photography offered by my friend Jack Milchanowski. He is an award-winning photographer, and I have enjoyed his professional expertise and his friendship over the years.

A special thank-you is owed to Ms. Myrna Richley, who provided valuable family information and documents for my story relating to the Border Wars of Kansas and Missouri during and following the Civil War.

My sincere appreciation must also go to Deb Bierman, who was most helpful while extending to me her time and information on my visit with her in Sedalia, Missouri. Her knowledge of the town past and present was so informative for this book.

I owe a deep sense of gratitude and appreciation to the loyal readers of my previous publications, many of whom have given me encouragement in this endeavor.

Last, I must thank Tate Publishing for their past and present work in bringing my last novel and this one to fruition in such a professional manner. Their skill and expertise are greatly appreciated.

PREFACE

Two objectives came to mind when I set out to write this novel. First, it must share the stories of my fictional characters with documented historic events and persons living on the American frontier between 1850 and 1890. Major events occurring during those four tumultuous decades have and likely will always have some impact, good or bad, on generations of Americans.

With my personal interest in the Civil War and past career as a physician created my second objective. That was to paint an informative and accurate picture of the practice of medicine that was taking place on the American frontier during and following the Civil War. My hope was for the reader to gain an increased appreciation for the outstanding achievements the practice of medicine has made since the late nineteenth century. Those achievements include huge advancements in medical education and knowledge, the creation of sophisticated scientific tools of medicine and their application, and the far-reaching research in biogenetics and development of pharmaceuticals of all kinds. Americans today are the benefactors when their doctors are using all of these for treating the ills and frailties of mankind with newer discoveries and technology being created daily.

During my research, I found a small number of inconsistencies pertaining to historical events that were expected. Special effort has been given to providing factual information regarding dates and events; however, I must beg the indulgence of my readers since I too may be guilty of omissions and errors.

When necessary, I took liberties for having my characters speak with the idiom I believed typical for the times. On infrequent occasions I also felt it necessary and important to employ journalistic bias-free language when I used the n-word to capture realism for the story. Its rare use was for helping to create that realism but still make a sincere effort to avoid misinterpreted judgments of my personal feelings that some readers might take from these pages.

The Civil War in our young democracy proved to be an especially defining moment for its people whether "free" or enslaved. Regardless of where one might live at the time, no one was untouched by the events of that war. I made every endeavor to make this clear.

While engaged in writing this story, friends urged that I include a few of my original drawings to supplement the story line. The drawings I have included merely represent my personal artistic impressions for each selected subject.

It is my desire that this book will entertain as well as enlighten its readers. I'm sure they will agree it was an exceptionally challenging and colorful period in our country's history, yet tragic and regretful in so many ways. Perhaps even more important, it should teach each of us that we must take away less from our triumphs and learn more from our mistakes and defeats.

Enjoy.

1

Beneath the dim streetlamp, a tall shadowy figure is seen staggering slowly down the city's deserted Market Street. At times, it appears the poor fellow is having difficulty just to remain upright. Since early evening, a steady and at times, heavy rain has continued to fall making the dirt streets muddy and more difficult to navigate. Frequent scattered flashes of lightning continue to dance across the black sky followed by intermittent loud claps of thunder, yet neither seem to give bother to the lone character slowly making his way down Market Street.

ooooo

The memory of that dark rainy night has remained fixed in my mind throughout my life. It had been a night of jubilant celebration both for me and several of my fellow classmates. On the following day, we would be graduating. Since I was quite unaccustomed to imbibing spirits, the unknown number of whiskies I had consumed during the evening hours had dulled my senses beyond belief. The Lord Almighty obviously had pity on me that glorious night in Philadelphia and helped me home to my second-floor flat.

I recall well my stumbling up that dilapidated narrow stairway to the dingy quarters I had called home since the beginning of my classes two years before. After fumbling for my pocket timepiece and then trying to focus on its tiny hands, I was mortified when discovering the hour to be just past 2:00 a.m.

It was about that moment when I also realized how rain-soaked my clothing had become during my sojourn back to the flat. I actually had some chill. After noting the hour, my dull-witted senses continued to inform me that I must get some sleep. There was important business for me to attend before the afternoon ceremony. That would include a lengthy walk to Lamberts down on Dock Street to pick up my graduation cap and walking cane. From there, I must continue on to Willard's Photography for my portrait. After finally getting myself into bed, I'm sure the whiskies put my mind quickly to rest.

My day of graduation was April 23, 1865, only two weeks after General Lee's Confederate surrender, which finally brought an end to the terrible war. By midafternoon on that day, my twenty-three classmates and I received our doctor of medicine diplomas from the University of Pennsylvania. When beginning our studies two years before, our class of 1865 numbered just over sixty students. A short time later, a number of the class left school to become volunteer recruits in the Union's Pennsylvania Regiment that had been actively engaged in battle since the start of the war.

I was born in the state of New York in 1840. Both of my parents were of Scotch-Irish decent. They christened me William Somers Watson; however, following my birth, I became known to everyone as Somers, with no one ever calling me by my Christian name. So throughout life, I have simply remained "Somers" to everyone.

Henry Clyde Watson, my brilliant but outspoken and caustic father, was a taskmaster. Oftentimes he was tyrannical while I was a lad growing up without sisters or brothers in our home. Father was renowned for his knowledge of the law and his burning hot temper. He had read law at the University of Pennsylvania, graduated with honors, and for ten years following graduation, rode circuit throughout the state tending to legal matters wherever his presence might be required. His tall imposing stature in combination with his frequent provocative personality brought him a well-known legal distinction, often feared by many. Later, he was appointed a district judge, and it was at that time when our family settled permanently in Philadelphia.

Lucy, my sweet loving mother, had taught school a few years before my parents' marriage. Mother's persona was much different from my father. With my being the only child in our family, Mother frequently intervened on my behalf when my father became too domineering for either her or her son to tolerate.

During my early youth, the eminent Judge Watson had already made plans for my life. His plan included my receiving the best education the city of Philadelphia had to offer, followed by my reading the law at Penn. From there, I was to follow precisely in his footsteps.

My dear mother's only plan for me was that I might eventually marry Penelope Miles, the gracious and beautiful daughter of a prominent and wealthy Philadelphia banker. My parents were in mutual agreement that our marriage would create a perfect bond for both families' political and financial future within the city. Throughout our growing years, Penelope and I shared a friendship, but nothing more.

Shortly after the beginning of the Civil War, my father began orchestrating all necessary arrangements for my entrance into Penn's law school. With profound misgiving, I dutifully began my classes to appease his demands. After six miserable months, I left school without issuing the slightest forewarning to either parent.

Following my unannounced and defiant rejection of the judge's plan and abrupt departure from Penn, he became immediately overwhelmed with furry and contempt for my rebellious actions. He promptly withdrew all future financial support and proclaimed his decision to my mother that I should be disinherited from the family, which brought much unhappiness and heartache for her. My rebellion had created an unwanted change within our family. Some time had passed before Father would or could accept the fact that his grandiose plans for his son had quickly disappeared into the air along with the smoke from his ever-present cigar.

With the persistent ambivalence my father and I shared during my youth, my admiration and respect gradually became focused upon my uncle. Silas Watson was Father's eldest brother, and exhibited a much different temperament. I had come to know him as a gentle, solicitous, and intelligent doctor. He was practicing medicine in the state of Missouri.

It was during my teen years when he and I began sharing letters and thoughts about many things. It was Uncle Silas who offered understanding and advice when I asked for it and when I needed it most. At one point, he suggested that perhaps I might consider reading medicine, but his well-accepted suggestion was a matter I chose not to share or discuss with my father. My thoughts about medicine were shared only with Uncle Silas since I was well aware of my father's planned future of study for me.

Several months passed before I finally came to share my early interest in medicine with my mother, thanks to my dear uncle. Without Father's knowledge, Mother began secretly hiding away money in a cache of savings for me. She began wrapping $20 paper notes inside several large balls of her knitting yarn from time to time. Perhaps her devious actions were the result of her strong intuition for what might happen later. I will never know.

The University of Pennsylvania's campus was located at Ninth and Market Streets in Philadelphia. Initially, only two buildings comprised the campus. It was without a library. My flat, also facing Market Street, was but five blocks distant from the campus. Penn's medical school was the first of its kind in the United States. For many years, its small medical faculty taught only by lectures what scant medicine each of the professors might happen to know at the time. Their limited knowledge had come without benefit of the long-established, highly esteemed, and sophisticated medical education at renowned medical centers in Edinburgh, Paris, and Vienna. Few students from America had the financial means to travel there for their education.

The subjects of anatomy, midwifery, and surgical theory comprised our major curriculum over the two years of classes although lectures were given that covered practice of medicine, anatomy, materia medica, chemistry, surgery, institutes of medicine and obstetrics. Fees were $15 and matriculation cards signed by the lecturing professor were issued to each class member. The reading of textbooks, when available on the fore mentioned topics, was recommended. Unfortunately, our second year proved to be little more than a repeat of the first. After successfully matriculating through the program, the student became eligible to receive his doctor of medicine diploma. Fortunately, our class of 1865 did benefit from a few significant new changes in the curriculum as a result of what had already been learned during the first years of the war.

Regretfully between 1861 and 1863, the Civil War had demonstrated that most doctors, whether serving in the Union or Confederate armies, were seriously lacking in fundamental medical knowledge. This deficiency became apparent both on the battlefield and in the hospitals. For the majority of doctors, their limited and often erroneous knowledge in most aspects of medicine had come from serving brief apprenticeships with aging physicians in practice. The older mentors simply passed on to their student whatever myths or misapplied and mistaken techniques they knew and had used before. However, the surprising duration of the war with its shocking number of casualties revealed how seriously unprepared most doctors were. It demonstrated that drastic and paramount changes must come.

Our professor of anatomy had great concern about this matter and was determined to have changes made at Penn's medical school. With political influence, he exhorted the Pennsylvania legislature to pass legislation that would permit the use of human cadavers for teaching purposes in our school. The legislature saw fit to approve the matter. Our class received and was permitted hands-on examination and dissection of cadavers coming from the state. The cadavers were a welcomed addition particularly for our classes in anatomy and surgery.

I took pride in knowing that I was graduating with honors. I was chosen to give the parting address on behalf of my fraternity, Phi Kappa Sigma, at the graduation ceremony.

For nearly six months prior to graduation, I had given much thought to what my future in medicine might hold. After receiving Uncle Silas's letter and his generous offer to join him in practice, I was overjoyed and determined to accept that opportunity and prepare for my move to Columbia, Missouri. Having never traveled outside Philadelphia, thoughts of moving to the Missouri frontier brought new excitement and anticipation. I was certain that practicing medicine out there would challenge me, and I was prepared and determined to accept that challenge.

ooooo

Silas Jenson Watson, barely past his youth and like many young men of his time, sought a need for adventure that had been burning inside his body. At age seventeen and with little money, he left home and family in New York. After working jobs in a variety of locations along the way, he was finally successful in arriving in Saint Louis, Missouri. There he gained employment on the busy flatboat landing docks that were bordering on the Mississippi River shoreline. He and fellow workers were responsible for stowing and offloading cargo being shipped to and from New Orleans.

At the time by a significant majority, his fellow dockworkers were slaves and were the property of the shipping company's white owners. While growing up in the East, young Watson had no previous knowledge of or dealings with slaves. After working with them on the docks a short time, he began having concern for the manner by which they were being treated by the hostile white supervisors. There were times when he saw them physically mistreated and abused. It was common to hear them being subjected to abusive and foul language. Silas thought the abuse and harsh treatment was being *inflicted* for little or no reason. He also recognized the few white laborers working beside him each day had little or no patience or friendship with the dozens of black men and boys. The slave owners and Silas's fellow white laborers called them niggers.

A brief period of time after arriving in Saint Louis, Silas met and promptly fell in love with Mary Ann Chester, a teacher in a city antebellum school, who was five years his senior. Just weeks following their marriage, Mary suddenly fell ill with what doctors called consumption. A brief time later, Mary Watson died of her disease.

While Silas continued to grieve over his wife's shocking death, his life suddenly changed forever one morning while working on the pier. While he and other hands were offloading a number of heavy barrels full of whiskey, one rolled across the platform striking his leg leaving a severe wound. A company owner rushed Silas to a nearby doctor's office for treatment.

The doctor was a recent immigrant from Scotland where he had received his medical education and additional surgical training in Edinburgh.

The young doctor's father was the eminent chief of surgery at the prestigious Edinburgh Infirmary. Stories about new opportunities on America's western frontier had reached across the ocean. It was those stories that prompted the young doctor's move to America. After his arrival in New York, he continued his travels west and settled in Saint Louis to begin his practice of surgery.

Over the following weeks while Doctor Stone continued with his meticulous care of Silas's wound, the two men developed a friendship. From the beginning, Silas had become entranced witnessing the surgeon's skill and knowledge. Prior to his injury, he had given nothing more than brief thoughts to his reading medicine or serving an apprenticeship; nonetheless, he now found the thought of it entertaining and exciting.

After days of willful thought along with growing trepidation, Silas remained hesitant if he should ask the surgeon if he might read medicine under his tutelage. Now filled with excitement and courage, he finally saw fit to make his desires known to the doctor. To Silas's complete surprise, Doctor Stone graciously accepted his request.

With fervor, Silas began study and work with his new friend and mentor. In only a short time, the Scottish surgeon had become impressed with his student's progress and dedication. Two years later, with the apprenticeship completed, young Doctor Silas Watson left Saint Louis filled with confidence and enthusiasm. He chose the small town of Columbia, Missouri, where to begin his practice. The year was 1851.

While Doctor Watson was engaged in and thoroughly enjoying his medical practice in Columbia, the 1850s across America were becoming a decade of progressive agitation and unrest. Two very different cultures were developing in the Northern states and within the Southern states. Their distinct differences were creating untold misunderstanding and discontent for everyone as it was gradually spreading across the entire country.

European immigrants entering the northeastern states were becoming largely responsible for cultural and economic changes being witnessed in the larger cities. A variety of rapid new industrial growth was taking place with diminished interest being given to farming as before. The North's population was also becoming twice that of the South. The growth of the North also created a necessary need for control of the expanding eastern rail system along with their heavy manufacturing.

In the South a much different picture was unfolding where major emphasis remained with agriculture and much less development and interest in manufacturing and industry. Significantly fewer immigrants were making a decision to settle within the Southern states. But, cotton was very quickly becoming paramount for the southern economy. The downy white plant was becoming king! Its presence on the market was gaining national and international influence and attention. Cotton was having and creating an explosive and dynamic effect on the South's economy. The basic fact was simple; in order to sustain such a ballooning economy, slaves were an absolute necessity for its labor force. With increasing numbers of slaves being brought into the South, their contribution and monetary value became unmistakably clear to everyone.

Growth of heavy industry and manufacturing in the North was having a mixed effect on each of its states' economy while dominance of agriculture, especially cotton, was providing the southern states an opportunity to make an extremely significant mark on the national economy. In summary, quite different problems and issues were developing in the North and South, and there was a desperate need for the federal government's assistance—and soon!

The states' representatives sitting in the nation's capital remained hopeful in solving many of the pressing issues with compromise; however, when attempts were made, solutions never seemed to be found. Always interfering was the pesky and daunting slavery issue. Sooner or later, it would sneak its tempered head into discussions on nearly every issue. Politically in Washington, it was becoming evident that views of the North and those of the South were becoming strikingly more and more divergent with the passage of time.

With the discord and indecision in Washington, nearly everyone's emotions were also becoming heightened across the country. People were becoming less tolerant of others' needs and wishes. America's beloved union of states was starting to crumble. The issues and problems in question were driving the northern and southern states farther apart rather than creating harmony for all.

When the individual southern states began to seriously examine how their smaller population was affecting their representation in Washington, they were decisively convinced they must be protected by rigid states' rights. Without them, they were fearful of Washington's passing legislation that would impose significant financial hardship on them. Such legislation could have a catastrophic affect on their present and future economy. The South was mindful that, at whatever cost, they must continue to keep all of their 4,000,000 slaves!

In 1859, with heightened passion and unrest continuing to grow throughout the country, an invidious and insanely fanatical northern resident named John Brown generated a very caustic and untimely campaign that soon proved to have grave consequences on the entire country. He publically rebuked slavery as a sin, and any person owning or using slaves should and would thereafter be considered sinners of the worst kind. His unsavory and mindless proclamation accompanied by the movement it created in public thinking brought forth immediate and dangerous hostility. It elevated even more the already heightened emotions within the South. The intense resentment his rhetoric brought produced for the South's residents a tighter bond for them, both emotionally and politically.

Later that same year, with Brown's continued insanity and fallacious rationale still working, he organized a small band of followers of like conviction. His group's revolting poor judgment and unquestionable ill timing failed miserably in their attempt to raid and capture a federal government's munitions arsenal at Harper's Ferry, Virginia. Their ill-advised intentions were aimed at creating a rebellion in deference to slavery.

After the rogue southern gang members were soundly subdued and defeated by the U.S. Army, fear escalated even higher throughout the southern states. Brown was captured, found guilty of treason, and executed. The Harpers Ferry fiasco had the South even more fearful and convinced of the northern states' plans to assume complete and unquestioned command of the government in Washington. Beyond any doubt, the South was now convinced that only after obtaining state's rights could they ever be protected in the future from unwanted actions by the federal government.

When South Carolina's shocking and brazen secession from the Union occurred on December 20, 1860, America had truly crumbled and had officially become divided. The state's fearless stratagem was followed within but a few days by the creation of a totally separate Confederate government having its own president, Jefferson Davis.

At 4:30 a.m. on April 12, 1861, the early morning quiet was shattered by the sound of the initial thundering explosions when canons began launching their munitions onto Fort Sumter located by the South Carolina shoreline. When those sounds were heard across the recently severed country, it became painfully clear to everyone that a war had officially begun. South Carolina's action that morning resulted from their furious opposition to having a federally garrisoned and occupied fort lying so very close to its shoreline. On that fateful morning, whether either side was prepared for a war, it made little difference. Now, no one could have doubt; war was underway!

As history would later reveal, the Civil War resulted in a much longer and more deadly struggle than either side on that April 12th morning could have imagined. For practical matters, it proved to be a bloody and extended conflict seeming to have begun by wealthy men but fought by poor men. Each president in the newly divided country was convinced that war was the only solution to America's problems and turmoil. But neither president realized how long and catastrophic it would become. Their estimate was ninety days.

During the months prior to that infamous April morning, each of the states' infrastructure and their residents were simply unprepared for the conflict that was to follow. Most Americans, including Presidents Lincoln and Jefferson Davis, remained confident the conflict would be very brief. Neither side had given any real thought as to what demands and obligations would be placed on them should a war take place whether it be materials and supplies, financial costs—or human lives.

Beside the many political issues faced by the north and south regions of America, the slave issue had slowly escalated and had become a matter of much greater importance than anyone had dreamed possible. The cotton industry had exceeded any and all expectations following the cotton gin's invention in 1793. The gin's presence in the South had remarkably revolutionized the production of cotton.

In truth, the issue of slavery had been slowly simmering in America's stew pot for several years, but was largely ignored by most northern and southern congressional leaders until 1860. Many northern congressmen had remained quite ambivalent and moderate on the issue, as did President Lincoln even following his election. Lincoln felt the federal government lacked the power to intervene.

Some scholars over the years have debated that had the slave issue never been present and had Congress been given sufficient time, their other nagging political problems would likely have been solved without ever going to war. No one will ever know that answer.

From the beginning, Missouri, Kentucky, and Maryland were declared and given the moniker "border states." In reality, each was a slave state, yet by very narrow margins each favored the Union politically. President Lincoln remained adamant in his belief that all three should remain firmly within the arms of the Union. However, President Davis was convinced that should those three states join the Confederacy, their presence would provide considerable assistance for the South's gaining their crucial state's rights. He was certain should that be accomplished, any effort by the

North to take them back at a later date would be very unlikely.

After the circumspect canon shots that rained down on Fort Sumter, the war's first legitimate military encounters actually took place in the state of Missouri. The state had shown little interest in seceding like South Carolina. In fact, Missouri had a strong desire to simply remain neutral.

Ironically, circumstances brought unforeseen changes. The then current Missouri governor held exceptionally strong personal sentiments for the Southern cause. Following this predilection, but unfortunately with haste and poor judgment, he foolishly ordered a garrison of his Missouri State Guard troops to encamp near a Federal munitions arsenal located on the edge of Saint Louis.

The governor's audacious plan was for members of his guard to launch a surprise attack on the arsenal, capture it, and then confiscate its valuable weapons and munitions. He firmly believed the capture of the arsenal would change political thinking of his state's residents so they would take sides with him and the proslavery group. After their change of thought, he was certain his beloved Missouri would and could willfully join with the Confederacy.

However, bad fortune was to follow for the mistaken governor. A bloody and deadly conflict took place on the streets of Saint Louis. Union soldiers put down the garrison's surprise attack quickly and were able to keep Missouri within its arms following the day's brief and convincing victory.

Thru the ruling of a federal law handed down in the 1850s, Missouri was officially declared the most northern state where slavery would ever be permitted. With civil war looming across America's horizon in 1860, that old law made it virtually inevitable that Missouri would come to witness major battles within its borders if and when war resulted. In the end, the state did suffer greatly over the issue of slavery.

With long standing personal wounds suffered by many of Missouri's residents inflicted on one another by their mixed political feelings regarding slavery, it was likewise inevitable that the already present and relentless guerilla warfare would continue during the Civil War. Unfortunately, vicious ambush attacks persisted during and for nearly twenty years following the war. While the senseless and often deadly ambush attacks were taking place around the state, 1,200 documented military battles and smaller skirmishes were making their marks on Missouri's soil during the war. Missouri was exceeded only by Tennessee and Virginia in total number of Civil War battles occurring within their respective borders.

ooooo

Following Silas's move to Columbia, his first office was a small space located on the ground floor at the rear of a General Mercantile store. Having little money, he was awarded free rental space in the two-story building. Townsfolk soon came to admire and love the new doctor and within a brief period of time he had developed a busy practice in the progressive and growing town.

Doctor Stone's excellent training gave Silas self-confidence while building his new practice. The skills and knowledge he had received proved beneficial for his patients in the years that followed. After Mary's death, he had no interest in remarrying. He was more intent on providing medical care for his patients.

Two years after beginning practice he purchased a spacious two-story house on a large corner lot that was surrounded by a decorative iron fence. The office occupied most of the ground floor while his private and comfortable living quarters occupied the second. His housekeepers' living quarters consisted of two small rooms attached in the back, next to the kitchen. A horse stable and wagon shed were located at the rear of the property.

While Civil War was threatening, most of Missouri's earliest settlers were small crop farmers having no slaves or particular concerns over the slave issue. As time passed however, many of the newer and more recent settlers were immigrants of German and Irish descent with most having significant opposition to slavery. The earliest settlers soon became outnumbered.

After working alongside numerous slaves on the Mississippi River barge docks, Uncle Silas's thoughts concerning the growing slave issue had become tempered over the years. But after living and practicing for several years in Columbia, he chose it prudent to remain neutral and made a point of remaining silent with regards to his personal views.

Like other states, Missouri was little prepared for what its citizens were being drawn into. In the spring of 1861 the first major military battle west of the Mississippi River took place at Wilson's Creek in the southwestern reaches of the state.

In December of that same year, after a slow, lengthy march in frigid weather, Captain John Velker's Union troops finally made their appearance in Columbia. On that blustery cold day, many of the captain's troops arrived shoeless and suffering from the rages of the terrible winter weather conditions they had endured during their long march.

Quickly, they seized and occupied buildings located on the university's campus for their quarters. While encamped in those buildings, their meals were prepared and served to them in various private homes throughout the city. This accepted practice became known as "war hospitality". With the Union garrison's arrival in town that cold December day, the city's population had suddenly swelled so it could consider itself strongly sympathetic to the Northern cause.

4

Silas issued a huge sigh as he leaned back in his chair and glanced across his paper-strewn desk. While alone in his office, he had become lost in deep thought about what events the future days would bring. His office and home had been comfortable and served him well for nearly twenty years. With sadness and foreboding, the doctor was contemplating the enormity of now leaving his beloved wife, his home, and his patients the following day.

Like most doctors throughout the newly divided country, Silas Watson felt an obligation to volunteer his service to the needs of the soldiers whether from the Union or the Confederacy. Until this time, Silas had kept his pent-up ambivalent feelings to himself regarding several issues, one of which was slavery. Those feelings had continued giving him some reluctance even to the previous day when he had officially signed to volunteer serving in the Union Army.

"Would you like a cup of tea, my dear?" Idabel inquired as she made a sudden appearance in his office doorway.

Now with his scattered thoughts suddenly interrupted by his wife's presence, he responded, "That would be wonderful, sweetheart." Light coming through the doorway was creating a statuesque shadow of her being cast upon the wall across his small office. Silas turned in his chair to gaze at his beautiful young wife standing before him attired in her long nightdress.

After the shocking death of his first wife, Silas had remained heartbroken, and for years, he had remained steadfast against any thought of a second marriage. Instead, he had chosen to remain in his home and office on Ninth Street with little thought of ever changing his adapted lifestyle. With his grief beginning to dispel over time, he had come to enjoy his solitude and independence.

Like several merchants in town and soon after he acquired his office and home in Columbia, Silas employed a married nigger couple to assist with his daily needs around the property. For years, Cele and his jovial and energetic wife, Lena had maintained their private quarters in the two small rooms next to the kitchen. They had remained his faithful housekeepers and loyal friends. The doctor paid them well and always enjoyed their company and the kindness they bestowed him. In return, he maintained close watch over the older couple and provided for their every need, whatever that might be.

Cele tended the large garden and yard as well as the stable that housed the doctor's two horses. Each day with Cele's help, Lena meticulously performed her housekeeping chores. She prepared savory meals for the doctor, most often with items Cele had taken from their garden or preserves the couple had jointly prepared and stored for the winter months.

After first meeting Idabel Turner one evening at a civic stage play held in a local theater, the beautiful young woman had brought a new meaning for Silas Watson's busy life. Already in his late forties, the doctor was deeply affected by the mature young woman of just nineteen years. A romantic attraction was nurtured shortly after their first meeting, and just one month later, the smitten and happy doctor had asked the adorable Idabel for her hand in marriage.

On this particular evening while seated in his partially darkened office, he pondered over the joyous six months since their marriage. Silas savored the newfound love and happy days Idabel had given him. He was certain his leaving tomorrow would be very difficult for both of them.

"Here's your tea, Silas," she said with a smile while placing the cup and saucer on the corner of his desk, then turning and placing a tender and sensuous kiss atop his forehead. The love the couple had already shared with its contentment and peace had been evident to everyone from the beginning of their marriage. When turning to leave, she added softly, "I'm going up to bed and read a few Bible passages."

While Silas could only imagine how much he would miss his wife in the days to follow, he was confident like everyone that the war would be of short duration. The doctor had solace in knowing that Idabel would remain in the capable hands of Cele and Lena during his absence.

ooooo

When Dr. Watson volunteered his professional service for the Union cause, only 115 officers could be counted in its army. Of that number, twenty-seven resigned and walked home after the first outbreak of hostilities. Unlike most volunteer doctors, Silas was offering years of experience with surgical skill. By necessity, the medical corps numbers were rapidly expanded in light of the unexpected number of war casualties.

After only a brief time following his entrance into the army, Silas discovered that enemies more dreadful and sinister than bullets were lurking in the corners of every camp—disease and ignorance. He was astounded when discovering the lack of knowledge and plain ignorance of doctors. Most had been trained as an apprentice much like himself, yet his work with the Scottish surgeon had given him skill, knowledge, and experience that far exceeded others when treating the casualties of war. Watson recalled Dr. Stone's oft-voiced criticism of the inadequate American medical training and knowledge. After observing the many inept doctors around him, Silas was forced to agree with his Scottish friend and mentor.

Both Union and Confederate armies were poorly prepared in their scope of medicine and for the war's increasing duration. Lack of knowledge, inept organization and leadership, and a frequent scarcity or total absence of quality medicines and supplies brought unnecessary suffering and death for many fighting men. During the first year of the war, this critical absence of preparation would herald the foremost medical problem facing the Union and Confederate forces alike.

Few doctors could claim prewar experience in treating a simple gunshot wound or in performing major surgery of any type. Most had only trivial experience even treating minor wounds so when suddenly subjected to massive war casualties each day, most Union and Confederate doctors alike were simply overwhelmed.

In 1861 only two major military hospitals existed in Missouri—one in Saint Louis and the other at the military barracks just south of Jefferson City. With strategic river and railroad connections centered in Saint Louis, its military hospital became the most important one west of the Appalachian Mountains. In that same year the only other major military hospitals in the country were located in Washington D.C. and Richmond, Virginia.

Physician ignorance compounded by their frequent and unexplained apathy toward their work was often responsible for men accepted in both armies despite their preexisting illnesses. When these infected recruits were placed with healthy

men in already over-crowded quarters, their illnesses spread, often becoming rampant. Physical
examinations, when and if performed on new
recruits, were usually poorly performed. Of greater
importance, many recruits were pronounced physically fit by individuals incapable of ever making
an adequate medical evaluation.

Men coming from rural areas in the South
frequently had no previous exposure to common
childhood illnesses, therefore lacking immunity to
them. As a result, measles, scarlet fever and chicken
pox often ran rampant in the already unsanitary
and overcrowded Confederate camps.

Because of the poor organization and leadership
at the beginning of the war, doctors too elderly
for field service or those with little or no medical experience were mistakenly placed in charge
of larger hospitals where the most critical patients
had been transferred. Many of these patients died.

Silas was subjected to all of these unfortunate maladies of a civil war that should never
have begun. His surgical skills were recognized
early, prompting his receiving the rank of lieutenant colonel. Orders and assignments were issued
for him to provide medical care to the sick and
wounded wherever and whenever skirmishes or

major battles might occur. As time would tell, he remained within Missouri throughout the war.

ooooo

From a practical view the tools of medicine during the early part of the war were crude and proved inadequate and difficult to use. Doctors had two basic surgical kits available for use. The routine surgery kit was small with a few number of instruments carried and protected within its small rectangular leather saddlebag. Such a bag might contain a tourniquet, knives, scalpel, an artery hook, and a packet of surgical needles and thread.

The typical amputation kit was larger in size and contained several large scalpels, two or three bone saws, several tourniquets, two or three probes, curved surgical needles and thread, bone cutting pliers, and an artery forceps and elevator. The elevator was a flat metal instrument with a small scoop that could be used to elevate small pieces of bone.

Jacob Gemrig immigrated to Philadelphia from Germany in 1830. He was experienced in making knives and silverware. Several years prior to the Civil War, he began making specialized medical instruments. When the war began, he had already become a prominent manufacturer of such instruments in the Philadelphia area. He was awarded a contract by the federal government to supply surgical kits for the Union Army.

ooooo

In mid-July 1861, Watson was attached to the medical detachment of Brig. General Nathaniel Lyon's infantry divisions encamped near Springfield, Missouri. Lyon's volunteer divisions were growing rapidly in their numbers of men each day. His amassed troops would ultimately number nearly 6,000 men. While Missouri was trying to remain neutral at the time, severe tensions were already escalating between Union troops and members of the Confederate Missouri State Guard.

By month's end, a Confederate Arkansas militia had joined with the Missouri Guard amassing together 12,000 Confederate troops. The huge group was also encamped outside of Springfield. By August 6, the huge number of Confederate troops had marched north out of Springfield and then boldly occupied the wooded and rolling terrain bordering Wilson's Creek in Greene County, Missouri.

Meanwhile, General Lyon and Colonel Franz Sigel had combined their Union forces earlier also at Wilson's Creek. A fierce battle ensued with the Union and Confederate forces each receiving significant casualties including those killed, wounded, and captured. During the raging Wilson Creek battle, the Union Army's General Lyon sustained fatal wounds becoming the first general for either side to die in the young war. In the minds of some, his bravery at Wilson's Creek made him a martyr.

While stationed at Wilson's Creek, Silas was placed in command of a Union field hospital. The majority of his patients were subject to receiving projectile wounds from gunshots and rarely from light artillery pieces. Most of those wounds involved the extremities arising from rifles, muskets and small arms. Whenever those projectiles involved major joints of one or more extremities or had produced severe fractures, Silas was obligated, by the wound's very nature, to amputate the affected limb.

As the battle raged on in the field, confederate forces made repeated mass charges against the enemy, each time creating more casualties for the Union. Confederate recruits of all ages had brought from home their favorite old muskets and double-barreled shotguns. They took little time in demonstrating their experience and proficiency in firing those weapons and their excellent marksmanship. They kept a rain of bullets rattling and clipping the tree branches just inches above the Union soldiers' heads while forcing them to the ground for cover before ever assuming more secure positions. Back and forth across the creek, one could see and hear the *crack, crack* of pistols and the smoking and exploding blasts of muskets and rifles. The air became filled with the smell of acrid smoke and gunpowder.

By nightfall of that first day for many a young man, after first witnessing smoking gun muzzles aimed and then fired at them, their thoughts became quickly changed. Before leaving home for the war, whatever perception of war's glory and bravery they might have once had, by that first night it had vanished. When darkness began to settle over Wilson's Creek, most of the excitement of fighting the cussed enemy had also disappeared. Now the recruits, most having become filled with fear by now, realized they had tasted the bitterness of their first combat. For some, it was the first such experience while for others, it was not only the first such experience but also the last.

The stunning Confederate victory at Wilson's Creek assured the South at least a temporary foothold in the southwest portion of the state. Perhaps of greater importance, the victory brought reinforced sentiment and enthusiasm for the southern cause. Not surprising, with that enthusiasm came increasing numbers of volunteer recruits. When compared to the future staggering number of casualties the South would endure later in the war at multiple sites, the relative few sustained at Wilson's Creek had brought a quick victory at a small cost for the glorious stars and bars.

During the brief Wilson Creek battle, Doctor Watson's worst concern was for wound contamination coming from dirt, cloth fragments, and other foreign bodies with their likelihood for developing infection. While his surgeries usually proved technically successful, post surgical infection brought death to several with no available medication for its prevention. The Wilson's Creek battle was the first of numerous skirmishes and major battles throughout the state where Silas was called upon to provide service during the four long years of the war.

ooooo

Lexington, Missouri with its 4,000 residents was the county seat of Lafayette County. Its strategic location on the Missouri River gave it military importance. Many rural residents in the surrounding area of the county were slave owners with unquestioned interest in the Confederate cause. Hemp, a tall Asiatic plant of the nettle family, was grown for its tough fiber and commonly used for the manufacture of rope. The plant was a major crop being raised at the time in the Lexington area. Hemp, tobacco, and coal production were of paramount importance in the county's economy.

Several of the town's most influential residents were outspoken and always prepared to make known their views regarding slaves that were accounting for slightly more than 30 percent of the county's population at the time. Folks residing in the town and rural area, after hearing of the Wilson's Creek victory, helped reinforce Confederate sentiment and enthusiasm not only in the county but also in the surrounding Missouri Valley area.

The federal government had realized that Lexington was a critical site for retaining control of the important Missouri River waterway that was capable of transporting munitions, supplies, and the wounded. To gain and maintain that control, a Union garrison was stationed inside the town in July 1861.

After a somewhat surprising but very impressive victory at Wilson's Creek, the now vigorous and highly spirited Missouri State Guard with its 7,000 troops led by Major General Sterling Price, brazenly marched north toward the ever important town of Lexington. By the time Price had arrived at the edge of town, his volunteer army had grown in size to include over 12,000 men. The majority of his followers had consisted of both young and old individuals who at first merely tagged along but were later caught up with the enthusiasm and became voluntary recruits. Although many were naïve, they were still anxious to do battle against the Yankee's blue coats.

Price's men launched an immediate bold and vicious attack upon the small Missouri town. The huge volunteer army's gun muzzles grew white-hot blazing away at the Union's garrison. The thundering initial onslaught was followed closely with a nearly continuous barrage of canon fire. Employing both large and small canon balls, Price's men continued to drop them amid the outnumbered Union troops who were left with no choice but to retreat from the heavy pounding.

ooooo

Before the start of the war Oliver Anderson, a local wealthy pro Southern businessman in Lexington, purchased a scenic piece of property outside of town. A portion of the property comprised a picturesque bluff overlooking the river. Prior to the war, it was on that property where Mr. Anderson had constructed an exceptionally luxurious three-story home for his family. The very elegant and expensive structure had tall supporting cast-iron Corinthian columns positioned majestically across its front. The interior had multiple large elegant rooms, some with fifteen-foot ceilings.

Aware of the wealthy man's like of mind regarding the slave issue that he had freely and publically acknowledged on numerous occasions, a Union garrison moved onto the Anderson property soon after the start of the war. They arrested Oliver and then evicted his entire family from their home. The Union soldiers immediately transformed the elegant spacious home into a Union army hospital. At a later time, Mr. Anderson's political convictions caused his banishment from the state of Missouri.

It was early September 1861 when Silas received orders to travel to Lexington so that he might begin assisting Doctor Cooley at the newly transformed "Anderson" hospital. Well-known stories had circulated regarding the surgical chief of operation's long-standing penchant for daily imbibing of alcohol. Silas arrived on horseback one evening just before sunset along with a mule-drawn military wagonload of supplies. Accompanying him were five orderlies and a sergeant major to act as hospital steward. The orderlies were enlisted men who were to function as additional nurses while the steward would have responsibility for all hospital supplies.

On the morning of September 18, the first day of the Battle of Lexington, the Anderson hospital was already overcrowded with the care of over one hundred Union wounded and sick soldiers.

Exceptionally fierce and bloody fighting began for control of the makeshift hospital. During that first day of battle, military command and control of the structure exchanged hands on three separate occasions.

At one point during that infamous day, Colonel James Mulligan issued orders to his 2,700 Union troops to retake the former, and now besieged, Anderson home that had already received structural damage. But later that day, Mulligan made a senseless and untimely error. The decision he made proved costly not only for himself but also for his men. Immediately inside the dwelling's opulent entry hall, a tragic and senseless event took place.

Three Confederate soldiers, each of whom had already surrendered earlier that day to Union troops, were executed one following the other on the lower stairs that led from the ground floor to the second and third floors. The three cold-blooded assassinations on that stairway were in strict violation of a federal war conduct code.

News of the three men's flagrant murders brought immediate and strong retaliation by Confederate troops. On the third and final day, Colonel Mulligan, now also wounded, surrendered with many of his men.

Silas Watson was one of the Union men surrendering with Colonel Mulligan that day. Another shocking and mysterious event took place very shortly after their surrender. Silas and a small number of his fellow Union prisoners were abruptly released from captivity with no explanation. For Doctor Watson the three-day battle had not only been exceedingly dangerous but very stressful.

While battle raged out at the Anderson property, the Confederate troops in town were employing a unique and crafty warfare tactic. A small party of troops located then confiscated several large round bales of hemp. After thoroughly soaking each bale with water, the troops used them as a "moving breastwork" for protection while rolling them down the road inside the town during their headlong advance into Union gunfire. The Union's musket and rifle shot found their mark but only penetrated deep within the rolled soggy hemp. During their attack, none of the advancing Confederate group were wounded or killed while forcing the Union troops to retreat.

By the end of the third day of battle and their surrender, the Union troops had been soundly defeated and had sustained more casualties than the Southern forces. With the Union surrender the important Battle of Lexington was history!

After having suffered two consecutive defeats of major proportion in southwest Missouri, the federal government realized the necessity for improving their Union strength if they were ever going to maintain control of the state. In spite of added reinforcements, Union losses continued in several skirmishes and major battles that followed the Battle of Lexington. With time and countless men lost, the North was finally successful in keeping Missouri under control of the Union for the remainder of the war.

ooooo

With limited doctors available, both sides frequently found their medical personnel being transferred as needed from one unit and battle site to another. Silas Watson was one of them due to his surgical skill. After leaving Lexington, he was engaged with several major battles and a number of less important ones during the war. He served at Frederikton, Hallsville, Sturgeon, Rockport, and later at Centralia along Young's Creek. The Centralia conflict was particularly significant and bloody since the Union sustained many casualties there.

At most battle locations, his surgeries were performed inside cramped, unsanitary and over worked field hospitals hastily set up in tents or in some other available location capable of providing some degree of protection. There were occasions when a family was evacuated and their house utilized as a field hospital. In virtually all locations during the war, disease and infection from unsanitary conditions continued to kill more men than did bullets.

Routine "sick call" occurred early each morning under the direction of the medical corps personnel. Complaints coming from camp soldiers were first heard then followed by empirical treatment administered by the doctor. Whatever medicines were available on site were likely the ones used. Diagnoses were made by the doctor's intuition and little else.

Complaints of greatest frequency included either constipation or the more serious and frequent problem of diarrhea. All too often the diarrhea would lead to the much more serious and often fatal dysentery. It was a very serious life-threatening problem feared by every soldier.

Diarrhea affected nearly every new recruit to some varying degree. This frequent debilitating medical problem was usually acquired soon after the recruit's entrance in the army. Those significantly affected often became momentarily debilitated or fell victim to other diseases. The unhealthy diet consisting of poorly prepared and often spoiled food, cramped living quarters, and widespread unsanitary conditions proved the most likely cause. The dreadful and fatal dysentery had no known cure.

A variety of treatments were tried and used with hopes of reducing or eliminating this serious medical problem. Ignorant and poorly trained doctors would often times erroneously administer a strong cathartic that would just make the problem worse.

At sick call, other medical problems faced the doctors. Soldiers often complained of symptoms referred to as "camp fever". In reality it was typhoid fever and resulted from consuming contaminated water from any number or sources of pollutants. Malaria proved common and usually restricted men from being engaged in battle. For a majority of soldiers, sanitation and personal hygiene were simply unknown. For those men this ignorance often brought severe illnesses upon themselves.

Improper disposal of human excreta resulted in severe debilitating diseases in many crowded camps. With open latrines (usually called "sinks") being the norm and with occasional heavy rains, the excreta might, and sometimes did, get washed from the latrines into the camp's only source of fresh water.

To compound this problem of sanitation, there seemed to be a prevalence of exaggerated modesty among numerous men. Their modesty prohibited them from using the camp's open-air latrines so when necessary, they would relieve themselves of their bodily functions whenever and wherever necessary. Unfortunately, this problem only exaggerated the unsanitary conditions for everyone.

Medical officers sometimes showed lack of concern for the very basic of health needs for the recruits. Many soldiers would neglect to bathe for weeks on end. However, this problem was recognized and finally addressed by medical corps personnel. The men were strongly encouraged to bathe more frequently.

Since the average soldier had only one uniform or his own clothing from home, it rarely got laundered. If he did bathe, he usually had no recourse but to place his now clean body back into filthy clothing.

Civilian health organizations were formed to address many of the recognized sanitary and health needs of the fighting men. They were called "the sanitary commissions". Most often these new commissions were organized and run primarily by women remaining back at home. As the war progressed, they were found to be helpful in many ways.

ooooo

Historic records suggest that gunshots contributed to nearly 95 percent of battle wounds while artillery projectile wounds were significantly less common. Wounds that were derived from swords and bayonets were rare and usually found only within cavalry units. On the battlefield, non-extremity wounds involving the head, chest, or abdomen, with few exceptions, resulted in death. Few casualties of this type survived either the surgery or the inevitable infection that followed.

Munitions and the design and manufacture of weapons used by both armies were altered at various periods during the war. The old round ball fired from muskets had both poor trajectory and range. When striking an individual, they most often produced bone fractures of the extremities but did not shatter or comminute the bone. With the advent and production of the minié ball, somewhat different injuries began appearing with frequency.

The minié's weight was heavier than the round ball, but when fired from a rifled musket, its conical shape traveled with much greater velocity and accuracy. The minié produced shattering, splintering, and splitting of a bone upon impact and this typical bone destruction produced by what was believed more likely to result in secondary wound infection.

In some battle engagements, Silas spent grueling long hours at the surgery table performing amputations or other surgeries one following the other. On occasion with a large number of casualties, he might find it impossible to wash off his bloody hands between patients. On those usually rare occasions, the operating table was sure to become slimy with a mixture of patients' blood. Horrific scenes were sometimes present in those cramped surgical tents when severely wounded men were screaming out and pleading for pain medication or begging for their anticipated amputation.

Surgeons were heavily outnumbered by the sick and injured, and often dreadfully overworked. Reported statistics give evidence the Union had one doctor for every 133 men in the ranks while the Confederates had a much greater ratio. The South had one doctor for every 324.

Early in the war with the chaotic and poor organization of the medical departments of both armies, transporting the wounded from the field site of injury to the crude field emergency stations was severely lacking. However, both sides learned that the time that elapsed between injury and treatment was of essence. When treating severe wounds, the reduction in transfer time also reduced the chance for infection especially when amputations became necessary. Transportation of the wounded on mule driven carts or wagons proved to be of significant benefit in reducing that critical time period. Mortality rates diminished dramatically following that simple discovery.

Wounded soldiers, if fortunate and were found, were usually carried from the field by another person or by litter-bearers. Unfortunately, many were never found by anyone and their fate was more likely eventual death wherever they may have fallen. Two and four wheeled open wagons were used for transportation acting as ambulances. Transfers to major hospitals of the more seriously ill and injured were made by train when possible.

Surgical anesthesia, when available, consisted of both chloroform and ether. If neither were available alcohol in the form of whiskey was administered when necessary. The customary ether and chloroform also had their individual problems and risks. Each presented problems of safety for the patient, the doctor, and other medical personnel.

For their surgical recovery, patients routinely received morphine and other opium products, all being highly addictive. Ignorance and indiscriminant use of these opiates created major problems leading to high addiction rates seen both during and following the war.

Although medical officers were overworked and stressed, more often they found themselves with little or nothing to do that led to boredom. Those periods of boredom often led to frequent and indiscriminate use of alcohol that resulted in an exceptionally high rate of alcoholism among doctors.

Their typical day might include writing letters home or playing cards, keno, poker and other games—and drinking. Some relieved their stress and boredom by seeking the sexual pleasures of women whenever and wherever prostitutes might be available.

Considering their exposure to sickness, injury and death, the soldier's average monthly salary was $13.00. By comparison, a prostitute's fee commonly brought her $30.00 to 40.00 per encounter.

The bloodiest period of the war for both sides with regards to casualties was during the summer of 1864. This had a significant effect on morale in the northern states. Wherever found, hospitals were overflowing with sick, wounded, and those of pending death.

Fortunately, doctors learned a great deal during the war years, most often by pure chance and necessity. They learned that a cleaned wound with proper ventilation improved healing and reduced sickness. The scourge of diarrhea and fatal dysentery became less prevalent later in the war due to improved sanitation. Despite the gradual increase in medical knowledge and skills, mortality rates among the debilitated and weary armies increased. However, the quality, organization and management of the medical corps on both sides did improve dramatically throughout the war.

Doctors were receiving a great deal more medical knowledge than they had ever known before. In general, the practice of medicine had made great strides by war's end that would come to benefit all Americans in the future.

For Lieutenant Colonel Watson and his ten Union comrades, it was a frigid miserable night in early December 1864, less than two months following the massacre that took place at Centralia. Word came of developing hostilities in northeast Missouri. News of Confederate troops moving northward prompted orders for the doctor and his small contingent of medical personnel and infantry soldiers to move east to provide care should any significant skirmish develop.

The small mounted detachment was accompanied by a mule-drawn supply wagon. It was fortuitous for the group to have found shelter during the blustery night inside an abandoned barn. Each man had received some welcomed rest with having his bedroll spread out on a large stack of moldy hay. While hunkered down inside the barn, the temperature outside had dropped even further accompanied by blowing snow from gale-like northerly winds.

At dawn, the snow had subsided to only light flurries, but the severe cold and wind persisted as the men resumed their slow journey. In single file, they followed alongside a narrow creek bed frozen over with ice and snow. The small detachment's commander, Colonel Jasper Adams, had familiarity with the territory having grown up as a young boy in those parts. When the group had reached within two miles or so of the Cyrus Randall farm, the colonel sent a messenger ahead with orders for Mrs. Randall to have breakfast prepared and ready for the eleven cold and hungry men.

As the small detachment made its way slowly along the snow-covered trail, Silas tugged frequently at the collar on his heavy overcoat hoping to help shield his face from the bone-chilling wind. Nevertheless, annoying ice pellets continued to collect on his beard.

After the party had followed a sharp bend in the trail, the Randall cabin came into partial view. It was seen in a clearing partially hidden by large oak and maple trees. Despite his discomfort, Silas thought the setting picturesque with the tree limbs hanging heavy with snow and ice. He could see and smell the smoke rising from the Randall's massive chimney. The inviting view and smell from the cabin brought a renewed feeling of well being for each of the cold shivering soldiers.

While the group dismounted and secured their horses, the colonel made the group's arrival known to the cabin's occupants. The aging Cyrus Randall stood inside the doorway and welcomed each man into his home. The pleasing aroma of fried bacon and eggs had filled the large cabin while the soldiers took turns milling close to the massive fireplace seeking its welcomed warmth.

Grandma Jenny Randall was busy with the final touches for the breakfast she had been requested to hastily prepare. She appeared well into her sixties with long snow-white hair drawn back into a large bun. Her floor-length dress was covered over with a long colorful cotton apron.

While using her apron to wipe her hands, she exclaimed in a loud husky voice for all to hear, "Don't you men give any mind for showin' up here this mornin'. The Union militia has been here more than once, and they never did eat me outta house nor home, so you just enjoy the grub I fixed for ya." There was infinite pride registered in her voice.

Grand Dad Cyrus remained silent as he continued handing out mugs of steaming hot coffee for each of the unexpected morning visitors. An hour later, after expressing their appreciation for the welcomed and tasty breakfast, the soldiers resumed their journey east.

It was sometime before noon when the detachment happened upon a gruesome scene beside the trail. Clad in ragged remnants of Confederate uniforms and partially covered with snow, three soldiers were found lying near one another. Their frozen partially snow-covered bodies gave visual evidence they had been there for some time. Two were without shoes but had rags gathered and tied around their frozen feet.

Silas dismounted quickly and rushed to the side of a fourth man seated on the ground propped against the base of a tree. His cherry-colored frost bitten face showed a haunting mask of exhaustion and pending death. Flakes of ice and snow covered portions of his bared head and face. He also had neither shoes nor boots and both feet were likewise bound in tattered rags and partially covered with the blowing snow. He appeared moribund, yet when noting Silas now crouched at his side, he struggled in his attempt to speak. The involuntary chatter by his teeth kept interrupting his feeble voice.

"We g-g-got separated from our regiment... got lost. My men here w—w-were sick with dys-dys-dysentery...and have passed on...as ya can see. C-c-can...can...ya help me?"

Following Silas's instruction, fellow members of his medical group wrapped the helpless soldier's nearly lifeless body in saddle blankets and carefully moved him onto the supply wagon. One after the other, each frozen corpse was likewise placed on the wagon. With Colonel Adam's command, members of the detachment mounted again and in silence, slowly continued their journey east toward Kirksville.

6

With military battles and skirmishes of the Civil War beginning across Missouri at various locations, another much different war had its beginning years before within the state's borders. That war consisted of retaliatory, sporadic, and frequently deadly guerilla conflicts over one thing—slavery.

These vicious encounters began in 1855 along the Kansas–Missouri border. They later became better known as simply, the Border Wars. Self-willed and fanatical individuals, each having staunch mind set for or against the slave question, were the ones initially responsible for such conflicts. Later, their followers of like mind began campaigning to coerce their respective sympathizers into moving and settling in the Kansas Territory. Both sides shared the reasoning that whichever faction gained the greatest number of settlers in the territory would politically determine which side of the slavery issue the state would ultimately follow.

With brazen disregard, some northern states began releasing occupants from several of their prisons. The criminal's freedom was granted in exchange for their moving to the Kansas Territory. Chaos developed, and from 1862 until many years after the conclusion of the war, the guerrilla-type lawless warfare persisted in many areas of the state.

"Bushwacker"was the name given to the lawless, radical individuals fiercely committed to slavery and the Confederacy. Quite often, a great number of these radical individuals had loyally served their cause fighting in the Civil War. Others, having served for varying periods of time in the military, had suddenly walked away to begin a life of retaliation and crime on their own. Without provocation, these Bushwackers employed vicious and murderous tactics while ambushing and pillaging peaceful settler families and property. Often the victims may have had no interest or expressed any opinion regarding the slave issue, yet they came under attack simply because they were considered likely suspects for having sympathy with the North.

Conversely, the Kansas Jayhawkers raided, robbed, and killed whomever they perceived as likely or known Confederate sympathizers. Likewise, many of these men had at one time served with Union forces. Many of them, for their personal disgruntled reasons regarding the big war, suddenly had left the military to become lawless renegades. Similar to the Bushwacker, these individuals showed bold and radical views against slavery. They too sought revenge and murderous retaliation.

This despised, frightening and senseless warfare soon gained great concern by federal, state, and local governments as well as the newly formed Confederate government. The marauding gangs and their radical leaders became a serious problem to first locate then apprehend. In truth, control never did come until 1889.

ooooo

It was Palm Sunday afternoon, April 9, 1865, when the climax of the Civil War finally came. The distinguished and dapper General Robert E. Lee, dressed in his unsoiled and pristine gray officer's uniform, approached on horseback the previously designated vacated home with his aides at side. He slowly dismounted from his handsome horse and quietly and with dignity, entered the home's small parlor room. History was soon forthcoming inside the non-descript home of the previously departed McLean family. The dramatic scene scheduled to take place that afternoon was in the tiny community of Appomattox Court House, Virginia. The reserved and poised general remained in silence while continuing to wait patiently.

Shortly, a man of quite different stature and appearance arrived. Smoking his ever-present cigar and attired in a soiled, ill-fitting blue uniform, Ulysses S. Grant, commanding general of the victorious Union forces, arrived to accept Lee's surrender. The exchange was simple, congenial, and brief. Following a seemingly endless four-year war, it had ceased within moments by the stroke of an ink pen made by two very different men!

The war had consumed untold thousands of lives and removed billions of dollars from the country's treasury. For most everyone the conflict, beyond its earliest comprehension, became merely a thing to ponder with sadness after that afternoon in Appomattox. The most sagacious of men could little more than ask searching questions. And regretfully, they came up with few, if any, answers.

Chaos had reigned at the commencement of the war and it reigned again following Lee's surrender. Post war turmoil followed for the North and the South. Just like its beginning, there was total lack of planning for the war's ending.

Senseless and sporadic loss of life with some property destruction continued following that historic Sunday afternoon. Minor skirmishes continued at various locations throughout the country. Soldiers on both sides, now battle-weary and haggard, merely began walking toward their homes. However, there remained other radical and obstinate individuals who were unable to convince themselves or others the war was truly over. These individuals persisted in firing their guns until their last rounds of ammunition had been spent. In so doing, small skirmishes were created against bewildered and innocent believers. The Battle of Palmito Ranch became the final battle on May 12, 1865, well after the ink had dried on General Lee's signature for an official surrender.

In Texas, having previously seceded, there was now urgent need for protecting its Confederate property from autocratic confiscation by the post war federal government. At least half of the original Confederate forces in Texas had deserted or disbanded by May 27. Formal law and order disappeared in Texas and complete anarchy took hold in most areas of the state.

Adding to the problems in Texas, federal troops failed to arrive in Galveston until mid-June for their enforcement of the "new freedoms" for slaves and retaking command of the lawless state. In summary, the surprisingly long war was followed by an even longer period before the final peace came to America that was now supposed to be reunited.

7

When Silas returned to Columbia, he was a weary and worn man. The war with its dreadful experiences had created emotional and physical changes for him. On April 14, 1865, he arrived home after an exhausting three-day journey from camp on horseback. Wearily, he dismounted and saw that his horse had water and hay in the backyard stable before entering his home. He paused for a moment to have another look at his old familiar surroundings.

From the moment of their initial embrace, Silas detected a mysterious change in Idabel. For some unknown reason, she now seemed distant and almost melancholic. Her usual vivacious personality that he remembered so well now seemed absent. He became disturbed when noting these changes in his young wife. Their long separation had brought quite obvious and unwanted changes in his precious Idabel.

Unbeknownst to her tired and now confused husband, Idabel had only recently arrived at the most important and heart-wrenching decision of her young life. She planned to relate her story and decision to Silas, but it must wait until he was permitted a few days to relax.

Several days after arriving home, the doctor, with Cele and Lena's help, began arranging and making preparations for reopening his medical office once again. Still witnessing Idabel's persistent change in manner continued to bring worry for Silas. Perhaps if they started a family soon, it might be what they both needed and were missing! When the right time came, he would discuss his thoughts with her.

ooooo

"Massa Watson, Massa Watson!" came the alarming shouts from the bottom of the stairway. "Come quick, Massa."

Daylight was just beginning to creep through the Watson's bedroom window when Silas turned over in bed when hearing Cele's desperate call. "What is it, Cele?" Silas shouted back as he brushed back his lengthy gray hair and rubbed his sleepy eyes.

"It's Missa Watson. She's done hitched up the buggy and left in one big hurry. I dun not know

wheres she go in such big hurry this time a day!"
There was shear panic in Cele's voice.

Now fully awake and aware of the desperation
in his black friend's voice, Silas bolted upright in
bed and discovered his wife to be gone. With darkness still present in the room, he found a small
piece of paper lying on her pillow. He grabbed it
and rushed to the window so that he might read it
in better light.

In Idabel's written hand, the note read:

My dear Silas

Tis with a very heavi hart that i tell you
this and that i must now leev you. When
you were gone to war, two drunkin' soldiers
bursted into our house one night sevral
months past while Cele and Lena were
gone frum here. They attackt and violate
me, Silas, and they did it again my will. I
have now found I am with child. i cannot
bear this shame for you my dear, or for me.
You can fine me out by Conner's Corner.
May the Good Lord be with you alway.

With mi eternal love,
Idabel

Trembling and fearing the worst, Silas shouted to his faithful servant waiting at the foot of the stairs, "Cele, harness up Mollie quickly! We must go find her NOW!"

The frantic doctor threw on his blouse and trousers and pulled on the high-top military boots he had worn home. He descended the stairs and rushed out to the stable. Cele had already set the halter and harness on the mare and was nervously attaching Mollie to the four wheeled wagon.

"Massa, I jus' can't unnerstan' what's happnin'. I heard Gracie whinny, and I'd knowed it was her. I came outside 'cause I was 'fraid somebody was stealin' her. Dat's when I sees Missa Watson leavin' fast in the buggy with Gracie, sos I call you right away." Cele, with his voice laced with fear and bewilderment, described the early morning scene while making final adjustment to the mare's bit and headstall.

Quickly both men shared their place on the wagon seat. Cele grabbed the reins and gave Mollie a light crack of his whip. The mare pulled the wagon with its two pensive riders swiftly onto the dirt road fronting the house and headed towards Connor's Corner near the edge of town. Desperately, Silas tried to calm his fear for what they might soon discover at the famous country road intersection. He continued to whisper his prayer of hope as Cele guided the wagon swiftly toward their destination two miles distant.

Upon arriving at Connor's Corner, brilliant early morning sun was beginning to filter through the tall trees while casting its light across the adjoining roads. Cele drew back sharply on the reins, and Mollie brought the wagon to a halt. Some distance ahead, Silas identified his Gracie and her buggy-hitch. The black buggy was unoccupied and partially hidden on a grassy area beneath several tall trees. Silas jumped from the wagon and ran into the open area. Upon drawing nearer to the vacant buggy, what he had feared most came into horrifying view.

Idabel was seated on the ground with her back slumped against a rear buggy wheel. Her body gave no visual evidence of life. Silas quickly recognized his .44-caliber revolver still clutched in his wife's right hand. Trembling and overcome with grief, Silas drew closer and then saw the large bloodstain on her white nightdress just below her left breast. Idabel had committed suicide!

A soft early morning breeze drifted across the grassy opening as the sobbing and heart broken doctor sat on the dew-soaked grass cradling his beloved Idabel in his arms. While still seated on the wagon, Cele had taken in the entire calamitous scene in silence but with tear-filled eyes. He was witnessing two of the dearest and most respected friends he'd ever known. Now, one had left, but why? Uncontrolled tears began streaming down the old gentleman's brown and weathered face.

8

With the war over, restoration began taking place in towns and cities across America where the numerous canons had at one time or other inflicted damage in varying degrees. During the long conflict, Union and Confederate forces had relied heavily on what rail lines had already existed prior to the war. Each side had utilized the railroads for transportation of munitions, military equipment, supplies, and their wounded soldiers whenever and wherever possible. Between 1861 and 1865, new rail construction had ceased on the frontier and elsewhere, but by late 1865, renewed construction had commenced once again.

The Ohio River and the Mississippi–Missouri River complex were strategic highways of transportation during and following the war and contributed significantly to the advancing development of the West. Barges and steamboats carried foodstuffs, grain, and other goods to New Orleans and other lower Mississippi delta markets. By 1865, the establishment of land values across the growing frontier was based largely on the property's questionable access to one or both of rail and water.

ooooo

To my recollection, it was a rather chilly fall day in 1865 when I boarded my train at Philadelphia station for the first leg of my long journey west to Columbia, Missouri. I had been looking forward to that day with much excitement. I found it especially difficult bidding Mother good-bye. With great reluctance on his part, my embittered and estranged father did make an appearance but only waved to me in silence while standing on the train platform. I must admit harboring some sadness leaving the only city I had ever known; however, I was eagerly awaiting my travels outside of Philadelphia for the first time.

In preparation for my trip, Mother had purchased my train tickets and discreetly presented me with her accumulated and quite significant cache of money that she had so discretely tucked away in her skeins of knitting yarn. While frequently wiping away a tear, she tried to show a brave face while helping to pack my clothing and personal belongings in a large Saratoga trunk that had once belonged to my grandmother. For the journey, I packed a change of clothing and a few other items in a knapsack that I planned on keeping close at hand.

When the shrill sound of the locomotive's whistle pierced the air for the first time, I boarded and took a seat in one of the three available passenger cars. Knowing little better, I chose to sit on a bench next to a window. With it being my first experience on a train, I was uncertain what to expect.

Soon after our leaving the station, I began to sense a repugnant odor. My car was crowded with passengers, many with children. It became clear the car had poor ventilation. When several passengers farther to the front began opening their windows for fresh air, smoke, soot, and small hot cinders began blowing inside. Soon, annoying soot and smoke began to fill the car, quickly soiling passengers' clothing, mine included.

After my arrival in Pittsburgh, my rail ticket called for a transfer where I was scheduled to board a Pullman car. When purchasing my ticket, Mother had learned it was a new Pullman of latest design. The Pullman Company had named its new car the Pioneer and it would take me from Pittsburgh to the East Saint Louis railhead. When we were barely outside of Philadelphia, I was certain I would be finding the Pioneer more pleasing and comfortable.

As we lumbered along down the track, I had little notion what our speed might be. A gentleman across from me said our train was traveling between fifteen and twenty miles an hour. I tried sleeping but with little or no success. My irritation continued after having my freshly laundered white blouse already soiled with coal soot.

Trying to ignore the growing displeasure of my surroundings, I directed my thoughts to my long-awaited meeting with Uncle Silas. I had not been in receipt of a letter from him for some time. By the present date, I thought it likely he would have left the army and returned home. In his last letter, he made mention of how thankful he was for having survived the conflict without personal disease or serious injury. It also stated that he was looking forward with pleasure to my joining him in Columbia.

Once I had become accustomed to the rail car's noise and its continual to and fro rocking motion on the uneven track, I had also come to enjoy the infrequent but sudden blasts of the train's whistle informing us of our momentary stops in small communities along the route. The stops at small communities along the way permitted necessary refilling of the steam engine's boilers with water, the exchange of mail sacks, in addition to an occasional passenger or two.

After experiencing profound fatigue and body discomfort, I finally drifted to sleep nearly twenty-eight hours after leaving Philadelphia only to be jarred awake a short time later by the whistle. With burning and sleepy eyes, I barely heard the conductor passing through the car informing everyone that we were about to arrive at the Pittsburgh station. Drowsily, I gazed about the car, still not certain if I had heard correctly. Suddenly, once again there was the loud grating noise of steel against steel as the car's wheels grabbed at the tracks while bringing the train to its final stop. Despite my fatigue and weariness, with great pleasure I welcomed our arrival in Pittsburgh.

Peering out my window, I noted a platform of some length with large crowd of folks bunched together. Many appeared either anxious to be meeting someone on our train or excited and preparing to board another. Noting a much newer looking train sitting on a sidetrack, I suspected it to be the one I would board. I recall noting three or four men attired in regulation blue army dress milling among the crowd on the platform. I could only assume them to be pickets for the railroad.

After stepping down onto the wood platform, I took notice of the large overhead clock. Assuming it to be marking the official railroad time, I paused and readjusted the hands on my pocket timepiece so they might match. After making my way through the crowd, I entered the passenger terminal to check the schedule board. It showed that my Pan Handle Rail Company #3 was scheduled to leave in one hour. I was relieved since that would allow time to wash up and get something to eat. The long trip from home had provided me with a good appetite.

After taking lunch and refreshing a bit, I waited a short time on the platform for the whistle to bid us to board. After the whistle's first blast, I climbed aboard the elegant Pullman Pioneer car with my knapsack and settled into one of its much-welcomed upholstered and comfortable seats. I placed the knapsack on the floor near my feet and for a short time watched folks boarding my car. With heavy eyes and my need of sleep, I soon drifted off with no effort.

Having barely fallen asleep, I became conscious of a very pleasing aroma drifting over me. Its scent gave cause for my sleepy eyes to open wide. During my very brief slumber, an engaging young woman had taken her adjoining seat facing me. The Pioneer's design was such that it had adjacent seats facing one another to facilitate their conversion at night into separate berths. I became immediately enamored with her striking appearance as well as the beautiful fragrance of her perfume. There was little doubt she captured my undivided attention quickly.

Pausing for a moment and then with some hesitance, I offered my introduction. "Good afternoon, ma'am. I'm Somers Watson. It appears we will be sharing this journey together."

"I'm pleased to make your acquaintance, Mr. Watson. I'm Liz Cromwell. I'm going to Saint Louis. What about you?" she responded in a soft friendly voice.

"Oh, I'm also headed for Saint Louis and then continuing on west from there." I was unable to dismiss her natural beauty, which in truth, was beginning to dispel some of my fatigue.

After hearing the train whistle's three consecutive lengthy loud blasts, I was aware of our departure from the station. After traveling but a short distance from the station, a black porter attired in a freshly starched white tunic entered our car through its front doorway. He flashed a broad pleasant smile that was sure to show his pearly white teeth to everyone. He casually strolled up the Pullman's aisle and stopped midway. He turned and announced with a loud voice over the constant din of the train's noise.

"Hello, my frens, and welcome all of ya to our Pan Handle Rail Company's #3. My name's George, and I's will be your porter on this here car. As ya may already knows our train's gonna take us across West Virginia then on west to Bradford, Ohio. At ol' Bradford town, the track splits— one goin' up to Chicago town and the other to Indianap'lis and then on to Saint Louie.

"This here car's called the Pioneer and is spankin' new. We're mighty proud of it. We want each of you to enjoys your ride with us wherever you might be headin'. Later tonight, ol' George will be fixin' each of your seats into their special position for makin' up your berths. So don't you worry 'bout that. There's a toilet for men folks at the front and one for all the sweet ladies at the back. The parlor and dinin' cars are towards our engine in the front. Bedtime's at the eleven o'clock hour and wake up at six thirty in ze mornin' for all you nice folks. At 6:15 in the mornin' I'll come in and rings a bell to waken all you sleepy folks. I'm here to help you, so jus' remember to call on ol' George if ya needs anythin'."

After George's brief introductory speech, he turned and exited the car through the forward door where he had entered. Following his departure, noisy conversation continued among the passengers.

I paid renewed attention to Liz seated at my side. Now, with less hesitation but with some boldness, I asked if she would pleasure me in the parlor car for a glass of sherry to provide us an opportunity to become better acquainted.

She offered no comment, but with an approving nod and smile, she rose from her seat, and I followed her down the aisle. Upon entering the parlor car, we found it quite opulent. I felt privileged in having met Liz, and by now, I was already quite certain we would be sharing a pleasant ride to Saint Louis.

We shared a very pleasant conversation over our glass of wine. I felt obliged, but yet with some reluctance, to inform Liz of my inexperience with drinking spirits. I felt she should know that our meeting there, and especially my having a drink, was a special occasion for me. I also recall sharing my Christian name with her during our conversation; however at the time, I was disinclined to disclose the fact of my being a doctor. I merely left it that I was a recent graduate of the University of Pennsylvania.

Liz shared with me her life story. Her immigrant German parents had settled in New York City. Her father was a jeweler by trade. She was born in the City and was the youngest of four children. After attending boarding school, she began working in one of the city's largest general mercantile companies. Over time she had worked her way up in the company, but when a friend living in Saint

Louis had recommended her for employment as a governess for a wealthy Saint Louis family's three children, she decided to apply for the position. The current trip was taking her to Saint Louis for her interview with the family.

The father was part owner of a large bank. She was anxious to meet the three children and their wealthy parents. She held promise that she might begin work for them.

During our conversation, I noted perchance a gentleman seated alone in a far corner of the car intently reading a book. From where I was sitting, it appeared to me that his entire left arm was missing and the empty sleeve of his blouse was hanging limp at his side. My thought came to mind that he must be a likely casualty of the war. I judged his age to be a few years my senior.

After taking dinner together, Liz and I returned to the parlor car where I boldly indulged with another small brandy before retiring for the night. The gentleman amputee we had seen earlier was absent. By now, my unaccustomed indulgence in spirits in addition to my fatigue had made poise for my needed sleep.

After returning to our Pullman, we saw that George had everyone's berths arranged for the night as promised. I bade my new friend a cordial good sleep and crawled into the upper berth, leaving her the lower. My weary and quite relaxed body found the berth welcomed for certain. While drifting to sleep, I enjoyed the lingering pleasing scent of my friend's enticing perfume.

I recall finding myself wide awake with dawn's early light and becoming aware of the click clacking sound coming from our Pullman's wheels rolling along on the rails. At that early hour with none of my fellow passengers yet stirring, I was more aware of the sound. For the first time since leaving Philadelphia, I felt fully rested. With the continued silence of our sleeping passengers, it was apparent I had awakened before George had entered to ring his bell. After lying quietly for a moment yet wide awake, I saw fit to make my way to the dining car for a coffee.

So as not to awaken Liz, I carefully and quietly left my berth with my knapsack and made my way forward to the toilet compartment to refresh myself. Later, when I was about to leave the small compartment, I chanced to meet the gentleman amputee who was about to enter.

We exchanged a passing nod and pleasantry as I started to make my way forward to the dining car.

After arriving there, I found the car empty of dining passengers with exception of two or three who, like me, had been early risers. A dining steward ushered me to a small vacant table.

I took a seat by the window and immediately was captivated watching the changing countryside passing by my window. Its landscape was becoming bathed in the early light of a new day. Moments later, my attention was drawn to the tall gentleman entering the car with whom I had just met in the toilet room. As he approached nearby, I inquired if he would care to share my table.

While extending his remaining right hand for me to shake he responded, "Thank you, sir. I'd be grateful. Name's Waldo Jamison and what might be yours?"

I introduced myself as Doctor William Watson but urged that he just call me Somers. I studied the gentleman intently as he took his seat across from me. I found him to be tall, lean, and appearing quite muscular. A boyish face could not be missed beneath his heavy but well-manicured reddish beard and hair, yet I still believed him to be my senior by four or five years. His deep voice gave way to an unmistakable and distinct southern accent.

Waldo appeared to me to be self-composed and confident. He gave no hint of being awkward or clumsy with his handicap nor was there the slightest sign of embarrassment or his being self-conscious because of his affliction. I was impressed watching how easily he managed with his remaining arm. After giving the dining steward his order he asked, "Where ya headed, Doc?"

"I'm headed to Saint Louis first and then on to Columbia, Missouri. What about you?" While watching this man, I was especially appreciative for my own good health.

He paused for a moment still continuing to study me and finally answered, "I'm also head'n to Saint Louis. My sweetheart Donna Jean and I have plans on gittin' hitched up next week—that is, if she'll still have me! She's never seen me without my arm. I lost it at Shiloh. That damn Yankee minié hit me directly on my elbow. They moved me from the field to a big ol' converted hospital in some hotel down in Corinth, Mississippi. Soon as the doc down there saw what I had left, he decided to cut it off. Guess I was one of the lucky ones to survive Shiloh. I did lose my arm, but I didn't get that damn gangrene afterwards like so many others." Waldo spoke of his injury matter-of-factly, then questioned, "Where'd they have you durin' the war?"

I explained that I hadn't been in the war but was attending medical school in Philadelphia. Having the opportunity to observe and listen to the gentleman gave me to remember that as of that moment, I had witnessed but little in my life. Home and college in Philadelphia had been my whole world.

Waldo stared at me pensively for a long moment then spoke his mind, "Guess that makes you a Yankee, doesn't it? Hell, I don't give a damn what you are. That's all over now."

For nearly an hour, we were immersed in a personable conversation. We shared thoughts and life experiences with impunity. During our engaging conversation, a number of fellow passengers entered, took breakfast, and then left.

Watching Waldo made me aware that no soldier ever knows what the fortunes of war have in store. This man had paid his price of self-sacrifice for a cause for which, at one time, he obviously had firm conviction.

Without warning, we were suddenly pitched forward and to the side when our train made an abrupt and unexpected slowing. Our partially filled coffee mugs spilled over, soiling the white cloth covering our table. For whatever reason, an emergent application of the train's brakes appeared to have created the event. We heard the very loud bumping and crunching sound of each car's steel couplers jamming together in repeated succession. At the same moment, there was a sustained screeching sound coming from the heavy steel wheels grabbing against the rails beneath us.

I first believed we were destined to derail and crash, but then I felt ourselves coming to a halt. A quick glance out the window suggested that we were in a remote, heavily wooded area with gently rolling hills. I had little notion where we might be.

Our train had barely ceased moving when multiple loud gunshots could be heard directly outside our window. We immediately dropped to the floor for cover. With due caution, Waldo and I elevated ourselves just high enough to capture a quick glance out the window. Several masked men mounted on horseback were milling beside the federal mail car a short distance forward from our position. Their preemptive assail and actions on the train told us that an armed robbery was underway.

As we continued our pensive watch, Waldo's demeanor suddenly changed and he abruptly became visibly shaken. Registering obvious excitement, he urged me to direct my attention to a large dappled chestnut horse being ridden by one of the highwaymen. After my attention was drawn to the white markings on the animal's head, he informed me that such a "blaze" configuration was most unusual. I could tell those markings, which he was calling a "blaze" had created a great deal of excitement for my new friend. He then explained that the unusual blaze we were seeing was nearly identical to a horse he had once owned back home in Tennessee.

With my having little knowledge of horses, it meant nothing to me, but it was obviously important to Waldo. Two gang members kept their mounts and posted themselves with pistols drawn. Three or more men climbed aboard the mail car.

"I think that's the mail car they're gittin' into up there. If so, those bastards may be in our car next. Damn to hell, we don't even have a pistol on us," Waldo whispered, obviously mindful of our situation.

My mind tried to ignore his scenario, but I feared he was correct. Within moments, we heard the *crack, crack, crack* sound of guns being fired again only a short distance from our vantage point.

We were even more convinced the shots had come from inside or alongside the mail car.

A team of four horses and open flatbed wagon suddenly made its appearance on the scene drawing alongside the train. Moments later, three men began loading what appeared to be two large and obviously heavy strong boxes onto the rear of the wagon. The loan hitch-wagon driver remained in his seat and continued observing the robbery in progress.

The ambush in such a remote area had come as a complete surprise for the train crew. While watching the robbery take place, it was clear to Waldo and me that this was carefully planned and executed. The plan had been to steal whatever was in those heavy boxes. Having no weapons, our only choice was to remain in place and continue watching the events unfold outside our window.

After the boxes were loaded, I recall seeing at least four men remounting their horses and preparing for their escape. During the robbery, the two mounted pickets had remained steadfast in their positions. A gang member with horse at full gallop made his sudden appearance to rejoin his masked comrades. It appeared he had come from somewhere near the front of the train.

After two or three cracks from the driver's whip, the hitch-wagon with its stolen cargo bolted from the scene accompanied by the six masked gang members on horseback. With each rider spurring his horse deep, they made their rapid escape from the scene. After reaching some distance from our train, we could see them form a protective circle around the wagon. As we continued to watch, the group disappeared from sight over a distant hill.

The hands on my timepiece showed 6:15 a.m. We were relieved for own safety and having avoided any confrontation with the gang. Waldo and I each raised up from our position on the floor. At that moment, a panic-stricken member of the train crew burst through the dining car door. His facial expression made clear his alarm. He shouted out begging us to follow him. We followed and while we rushed from the car, he informed us that people had been shot and were in desperate need of help.

Once we had arrived inside the mail car, we noted a uniformed postal employee seated atop a high stool but with his upper body slumped forward onto a large mail-sorting counter. There were multiple bloodstains high on his back suggesting he had possible mortal chest wounds. I felt it likely he had been shot from behind. A quick examination confirmed my suspicion that he was dead and likely never saw his assailant. Blood from his chest wounds had already spilled onto the counter and onto several pieces of mail he had been sorting.

Meanwhile Waldo had rushed to aid a second victim that was lying on the mail car floor some distance from the tall wooden sorting counter. I heard mumbling sounds from that victim and rushed to join Waldo. I saw the stricken man's ashen face. It was contorted from obvious pain and fear. Blood was issuing forth from his nose and mouth while he was gasping for air amidst intermittent moans and mumbled speech. Waldo and I strained to hear his faint and labored words.

"The bank shipment, the bank shipment…they got it all." I noted the moribund victim to be attired in a dark-colored federal security agent's uniform. He was lying on his side on a thin cotton mattress, suggesting that he may have been assaulted and shot while asleep. His holstered pistol lay partially exposed beneath one corner of the mattress. From all appearances it had remained untouched and never fired.

During the coarse of my hurried examination, when I withdrew my hand from beneath his cotton blouse, I discovered it covered with dark blood, suggesting he too had been shot in the chest. The man was in extremis. Moments later, after making another attempt to speak, his glassy eyes opened and remained fixed. With a final loud gasp for air, he died. After further inspection, I discovered that he had been shot at least twice in the chest.

Word reached us that a third murder had taken place just outside the locomotive's cabin. During the brief time Waldo and I were involved with the shooting victims inside the mail car, the train's conductor and engineer were desperately trying to care for the other victim. That victim was the train's fire tender who was struck down by gunfire at close range while standing inside his coal tender car. He died immediately of multiple gunshot wounds.

I learned later that just moments before that assault took place at the front of the train, our conductor had been conferring with the engineer in the locomotive's cabin. It was suspected the assailant's intent was on killing the engineer. When the fireman in the coal tender heard the commotion inside the cabin, he had brandished his own small revolver. After quickly getting off an errant shot at the assailant, the fireman was fatally struck down by return fire from the masked man. The fireman fell dead just outside the door of his firebox.

After regaining some composure following the robbery with its three murders, our conductor began making an evaluation of the entire situation at hand. Three members of his crew were known to be dead with two being employees of the Federal Postal Service. The third victim was his long-time personal friend and valuable fireman and employee, Crandall Pinkerton. Fortunately, no passengers had been killed or injured, but now many were suffering from fright and anxiety after hearing of the deaths and robbery. The conductor tried to fight off his personal grief while retaking command of his train.

"We shared the conductor's grief and agreed with his initial impression of the tragic event. The ambush and robbery resulted from careful planning with advance information regarding the two strong boxes—the only target for the robbery. Information concerning the valuable cargo had to have been known and passed on prior to our leaving Pittsburgh.

The remote location near Ohio's west-central town of Bradford proved to be perfect for the early morning ambush and robbery. The small town

•   I I O   •

was one of the railroad's routine stops for water, cargo, mail, and passengers. With tracks taking two separate routes at Bradford, separate Pan Handle trains made their scheduled runs to different destinations – one to Chicago and the other to Indianapolis and Saint Louis. It was clear the gang that morning had prior knowledge of which train and which route from Bradford the desired cargo would be taking.

With good fortune, the engineer had been successful in safely bringing the train to a halt before striking numerous heavy timbers that were piled deliberately crossway of the track. The obstruction was carefully positioned at the south end of a trestle bridge that passed over the Stillwater River and near where it was joined by the smaller Greenville River. The heavy foliage and forested rolling landscape provided perfect concealment for the waiting gang.

How they acquired the critical information regarding the secret cargo was another matter and remained in question. It was sometime later when we learned of what contents were inside the two steel boxes. One strong box was filled with U.S. Gold certificates and numerous bars of gold bullion while the other box was filled with five, ten, and twenty-dollar gold coins and numerous bars of both gold and silver. Rumor had it that the stolen shipment was valued at more than $30,000. The strong boxes were being transferred from a large Pittsburgh bank to another in Indianapolis. By prearranged plan, a uniformed federal security agent had been assigned to accompany the shipment and issued instructions to remain at all times with the cargo for the entire trip to Indianapolis.

With the volunteer assistance from several passengers, members of the train's crew were able to remove the heavy timbers from the tracks. The bodies of the three murdered men were wrapped in bed sheets and placed side by side on the floor of the postal car.

Members of the crew passed through each passenger car hoping to calm the anxious passengers and provide them with limited details of the robbery. After a two-hour delay, I was aware of our train's slow movement as we began crossing the trestle bridge and then continued on our way to Bradford. The new day had not started well for everyone aboard the Pan Handle #3.

10

As our train gained speed and continued on its journey to Bradford, Waldo and I returned to our Pullman noting that both dining and parlor cars had become crowded with noisy passengers filled with excitement about the early morning events. My concern had returned to Liz and how she had withstood the early morning turmoil. We found our car nearly empty of passengers.

The privacy curtain for Liz's lower berth was parted slightly. I could see she was fully dressed and lying on her unmade berth. Uncertain if she might be sleeping or ill, I hesitated a moment before reaching through the curtain and touching her shoulder. When hearing and recognizing my voice, she turned over and faced me.

"Good morning, Liz. With this morning's excitement, I was mindful if you were all right. I awoke early and hoped I wouldn't disturb you. My friend and I were having coffee in the dining car when the train was ambushed and robbed of some cargo."

She looked up at me with a smile and said, "I'm grateful for your interest and kindness. I was jolted awake with the train's sudden stop and then became frightened when hearing the gunshots. I had no idea what might be happening. I felt it best that I remain in my berth. What have you been doing?"

Before I could respond, Waldo appeared at my side and answered for me, "Doc and I were asked to check on the two men that were gunned down in the mail car."

I trusted that Liz had missed hearing Waldo's reference of me as Doc. Liz quickly parted the privacy curtain and sat upright. Now with vested interest registered in her voice, she asked, "Did I hear him correctly? Is it true that you are a doctor?"

I was hard-pressed to answer with veracity. "Yes Liz, I just graduated from medical school in Philadelphia and have plans to join my uncle's practice out in Missouri."

Brushing back her blond hair, she responded somewhat bashfully, "That means I'm obliged to call you 'Doctor' and *not* just Somers. May I pay my regards for your achievement, Dr. Watson!"

"Please, I'm still just Somers to you. Let's go take some breakfast now. By the way Liz, please make your acquaintance to my friend, Waldo. Suffice it to say, he and I have encountered a vast more bit of excitement than we had plans for this morning."

After finding vacant seats in the dining car, Waldo began relating the saga of our morning experience. Liz listened intently to his every word. While taking breakfast, we heard three separate loud blasts coming from the train's whistle indicating our arrival in Bradford. Everyone had been anticipating an extended delay while there so as to permit the train's crew to mind the urgent business that lay at hand. I wondered if Waldo and I might be questioned regarding the two murdered men we were requested to check on. I had some trepidation as to what may lay ahead for us.

When we stepped from the train, the railroad clock inside the depot showed it to be 10:00 a.m. A loud announcement was issued that all passengers continuing on to Indianapolis and Saint Louis should return on board before twelve noon.

The depot building's small dining chamber had quickly become overcrowded with noisy passengers who had not taken breakfast earlier. We chose to find a quiet place for passing away time before our noon departure. Since Liz was unable to eat while on the train, the three of us set out to find her some breakfast elsewhere.

While leisurely walking up the road leading through Bradford, a handsome two-story hotel building on a nearby street corner came into view. We could see a livery stable and blacksmith's forge and shop next door to the hotel. As we approached closer, Waldo was awestruck when seeing a lone horse standing tied at a hitch-post just outside the hotel entrance.

After deliberate scrutiny of the animal, it immediately dispelled any doubt in Waldo's mind. It was exactly the same large chestnut mare he'd seen that morning outside the train window during the robbery. And the white blaze was identical.

My visibly excited friend cried out, "My god, Somers, that's the same filly I pointed out to you this morning."

The horse was still carrying its saddle and headstall. With due care, Waldo gently approached the mare all the while talking softly to her. He rubbed his hand gently across her flank and then withdrew it so that I might also witness the mare's sweat that was now present on his palm and fingers.

With rapt excitement, my friend continued to rant, "This horse has been ridden hard and recently, by damn! Just look again at her blaze. It's the very same one I pointed out to you before. By god, I'll bet her rider is somewhere inside this damn hotel right now."

I could not dispute Waldo's conclusion as he turned abruptly and started for the hotel entrance with Liz and me following close behind. Waldo's knowledge of horses had convinced me by now this was indeed the same horse we had seen before. As we entered the hotel, I could only guess what would come to pass as I kept watch on my obviously aroused southern companion.

We found the lobby of the hotel small and quite ornate with an extra-high ceiling. As I looked around, I could tell it to be quite elegantly appointed. We approached an elderly clerk seated behind a handsomely carved wooden desk. The old gentleman was engrossed reading his newspaper and displayed no special interest with our presence. He was slight of build and after finally looking up from his newspaper, his spectacles slipped far down on his long slender nose.

Now peering above them and noting Waldo and I accompanied by a very attractive young woman, he grinned and offered a snide greeting, "And a very good mornin' to the fair lady and also to both of you gents. Let's see——are we in need of just a single or more than one room this fine day?" Then with another wry grin, he gave a broad mischievous smile and wink directed at each of us.

Attempting to forebear the clerk's cunning and discerning comments, Waldo inquired pointedly, "Do you have a guest or have ya seen the person whose mare is hitched out front?"

The clerk abruptly altered his once friendly facial expression while answering in a brusque manner, "Don't you make mind of that horse, mister. My young hosteler will be back shortly to take care of her. Our guest just registered a short while ago saying he'd just had a hard ride this mornin' and wanted his horse fed and watered while he caught a few hours rest."

I could tell Waldo was becoming perturbed when the pitch of his voice elevated. "Is your marshal around? We must talk with him. We've jus' arrived on that train down at the depot. Earlier this mornin', a gang of masked hoodlums robbed the train and murdered three men in cold blood. Now my friend and I just recognized that filly tied up outside your hotel. Mister, we damn well know that horse and its rider were involved with the robbery, so it's important that we talk with the marshal *now*."

Somewhat taken aback yet displaying no undue interest in the entire matter, the clerk said, "If what ya say is so, the marshal's probably already down by your train askin' folks questions."

Waldo's voice was starting to show frustration and conviction, "I'm here to tell ya, mister, that guy you just sent to one of your damn rooms for his nap is most likely one of the bastards that murdered those poor men on the train!"

At that moment, a young boy, probably short of twelve years, entered the lobby. Seeing his hosteler, the clerk instructed, "Robert, run down to the depot and try to find the marshal for these anxious travelers. If he's down there, ask him to hurry up here as I've got these folks here that are on edge and say they need to talk with him right away." The boy offered no reply but rushed out the door to look for the town marshal.

While Liz was taking breakfast in the hotel's small dining room, Waldo and I kept close watch on the mare. We shared concern if the horse's owner might suddenly descend the stairs having decided on a much shorter nap than he had once planned.

Time passed slowly while waiting in the lobby for the marshal's arrival. Suddenly, the stable boy burst through the door out of breath and filled with excitement after learning of the train robbery. Robert informed the clerk he had found the marshal and that he was on his way. The boy rushed back outside to attend the mare that was still awaiting her promised water and hay.

The man entering the hotel lobby was straight and tall like a large oak tree. Standing well over six feet and appearing of middle age, his chiseled facial features displayed a large thick graying mustache with both ends curled upward. His hair was quite long and falling over his collar. A marshal's badge of shiny silver was attached to the lapel of his well-worn leather vest. His appearance was commanding in every way as he approached his town's three anxious visitors.

Immediately showing his respect to Liz, he removed his wide-brimmed hat, then spoke with a deep resounding voice, "I presume you are the folks that have information for me about the robbery and killins', is that right? My name's Barlow, and I'm the marshal 'round here. What can ya tell me?"

After meeting the man, there remained little doubt in my mind that Barlow was a seasoned and serious lawman. He gave the impression of being all business with little interest in idle talk. Barlow wore a heavy gun rig secured about his waist. I was also sure he knew how to use it.

My excited companion began enlightening marshal Barlow immediately about our observations. "The three of us were passengers on the train at the time of the holdup this morning. While having coffee in the dining car, my doctor friend and I got a close look out the car window at most of the men in the gang and some of their horses. I made comment to the doctor about the unusual white blaze on a large dapple chestnut mare since it closely resembled a horse I once owned. Lo and behold, we arrived here a while ago and spotted that same horse tied out front and damn wet with a heavy sweat worthy of a very recent hard ride."

I spoke up and added, "The clerk informed us he had just signed in a person who had arrived a short time ago on that horse. The gentleman is likely taking rest in one the hotel's rooms as we speak. We enjoin you to question the guy 'cause we are most assured he was one of the gang members who may have shot two men inside the train's postal car."

Barlow became increasingly attentive to our story. "I will find out where Jake put the guy and awaken him for a little chat. Thanks for the obliging tip." With that said, the lawman returned his hat upon his head and approached the clerk's desk to learn the guest's room number. As we left the hotel, the marshal was last seen climbing the wide curving stairs leading to the hotel's second floor.

By noon, the train's passengers had returned to their places. With haste, information ascertained from the conductor and engineer was telegraphed to each of the involved banks, the offices of the Pan Handle Railroad Company, and the offices of the Federal Postal Service.

In due course, word had circulated throughout the small town's citizens creating excitement and a swirl of conversation in a community unaccustomed to such activity. A substitute postal worker assumed his position in the mail car for the trip to Indianapolis while a local volunteer assumed the deceased fireman's position in the tender.

Pan Handle #3, now hopelessly disrupted from its normal operating schedule, left Bradford with the depot clock's hands pointing to 12:35 p.m. The morning's ordeal with its delays had upset some of the passengers, but all remained thankful no one else had been killed or injured. For many, their thoughts and prayers were now with the families of the three slain men.

After a second unexpected lengthy layover in Indianapolis, an additional night was required aboard our Pullman before our reaching Saint Louis. After finally arriving at the large East Saint Louis railroad yard shortly before noon the following day nearly, everyone was showing evidence of the long weary trip.

While stepping off the train we were met with a cool drizzle of rain. Meeting face-to-face in silence on the wet platform, neither Liz nor I was anxious to part nor did we have words to explain our feelings for each other that we had quite obviously acquired over the previous days together. Unknown to us that day, those special moments standing in the rain on the train platform would remain fixed in our minds for a very long time. We had reason to believe we might never meet again. Our developing relationship had made the long trip from Pittsburgh enjoyable for each of us. Before parting, we shared a prolonged tender and passionate embrace.

Before parting, we wished Waldo much happiness with his forthcoming marriage and for his new home in Saint Louis. With waves and goodbyes to one another, we went our separate ways and disappeared amidst the noisy crowd.

While securing my trunk from the baggage car, my thoughts remained with the beautiful young woman from whom I had just parted. With Liz now gone, I now realized I had begun having special feelings for her—feelings I had never shared or experienced with any woman before.

11

It was several weeks before the end of the war when I had last had any letter from my uncle. That last correspondence came while he was still serving in the Union army somewhere in Missouri. The letter indicated his hope for the war to end soon so that he could return to his wife and practice in Columbia.

After the tiring long trip from Philadelphia, I made the decision to remain overnight in Saint Louis before continuing my journey on the Concord Stage line to Columbia. I knew I would welcome the extra rest.

Early the following morning after taking breakfast, I packed a small snack to take with me for lunch while on the stage later in the day. I watched as the stagecoach driver and his assistant loaded and secured my trunk atop the red colored carriage along with an assortment of cargo and baggage belonging to fellow passengers. I had been looking forward to this part of my long journey since I had never ridden in a coach of any kind. I was also anxious to see new areas of the frontier; ones I had only heard about in stories.

A blazing sun was bearing down on us as our coach rumbled and swayed along the dusty and bumpy road west of Saint Louis heading for Columbia. My fellow occupants and I were continually jostled in the swinging and swaying coach. A continual hot breeze and torrent of dust swirled inside the coach's open windows. The team of six stout horses drawing our coach was scheduled for exchange for fresh animals about every ten or so miles at small "swing stations" along the route to Columbia.

My travel companions included a young mother with a small baby in arms, a young girl probably of fourteen years, and an older gentleman that immediately caught my attention shortly after we had boarded. Only the baby was able to sleep during the rough ride.

The baby's mother seemed to be a plain, quiet woman with evidence of a motherly good nature. She was attired in a neat brown calico dress with matching bonnet. The girl's long blond hair fell in curls below her bonnet. She was also wearing a long colorful dress. The baby's mother and I began sharing a friendly conversation while the young girl's shyness limited her conversation.

I studied the older gentleman trying to make reason for his unnerving and peculiar behavior I had been noting since our leaving Saint Louis. He was shabbily attired and wore a heavy unkempt gray beard. I guessed his age to be in the late 50s or early 60s. He maintained a withdrawn and mysterious silence showing little or no interest in joining our conversation. He appeared morose and restless and continued to fidget in his seat.

Mother and baby along with the young girl had plans for continuing their travels to Kansas City. The farther we continued on our journey, our strange travel partner grew progressively more nervous and agitated. As we approached ever closer to the "home station" stop in Warrenton where we could exchange horses and have an opportunity to stretch our legs, I found it peculiar how he was repeatedly turning in his seat to peer out the open window as if continually questioning our current whereabouts.

On one occasion, I noted a small derringer pistol partially exposed in the waist of his soiled trousers. Since leaving Saint Louis, he had frequently removed a small container of whiskey from his coat pocket. Each time after taking in a deep swallow, it was returned to his pocket for safekeeping. It was difficult for me to tell if his glazed deeply reddened eyes had come from whiskey or the thick dust that continued intermittently to fill our coach.

When our stage driver pulled back hard on the team's reins, the horses responded with a gradual slowing of our coach. I could hear the scraping noise as the assistant applied pressure to the brake lever finally bringing the coach to a halt outside a small wooden building that I discovered later to be serving as Warrenton's temporary post office. Our coach became enveloped in a huge swirling cloud of dust after stopping with much of it finding its way inside our compartment.

Located behind the building, I noticed an enclosed pen containing several fresh horses ready for exchange. I was hoping this stop might be sufficiently long enough for me to eat the small lunch I had brought with me.

With no forewarning, our obviously disturbed passenger suddenly jerked the derringer from his waist, swung open the coach door, and jumped down from the stage. Moments after he disappeared inside the building, we heard the loud *crack* of a single gunshot.

The gun's report awakened the baby and brought an excited response from several horses in our team hitch while waiting to be released from their harness for the exchange to take place. The young girl screamed out in fright when hearing the gunshot, and the frightened mother quickly tried to calm her now disturbed and crying infant.

As the assailant attempted to make his escape from the building, the stagecoach guard got off two thundering shots from his carbine that brought down the fugitive a few yards from the building. The loud blasts from the carbine brought repeated nervous excitement for the horses in our hitch and those fresh ones waiting in the pen. I leaped from the coach as did the guard and rushed inside the office.

We found a wounded postal clerk lying on the wooden plank floor. He had taken a single hit from the derringer in his right shoulder. He was conscious but moaning with pain. With a cursory examination I could find no other wounds. I was unable to find an exit wound and had to assume the slug remained buried in the fleshy part of his shoulder. My immediate conclusion was that he did not appear to be in any mortal danger.

The stage driver had left his seat and rushed down the street to a nearby saloon for help, while back inside the post office, I was making the wounded man as comfortable as possible. It was then when I began to question him.

"Did you know this guy that shot you?" I asked.

"Yeah. Name's McHenry. He's been a bushwacker and group leader of some pro-Southern guys back durin' the war. He used to live 'round here, but I hain't seen him for a good spell. Guess he hasn't heard the war's over."

"Why was he after you?" the guard asked.

"Most probably 'cause I shot his brother out at the edge of town during the last week of the war. That Herman McHenry guy was good for nothin' just like his brother that jus' shot me. I caught Herman tryin' to steal my two horses."

Several men suddenly appeared outside the doorway, all appearing excited and anxious to learn more about the shooting incident. The group of local onlookers had accompanied the deputy marshal who first confirmed the assailant lying outside on the ground to be dead. The deputy then entered the small building to question and check on the wounded postal clerk.

•   1 3 0   •

When he saw the stagecoach guard and me standing over the wounded man, the deputy introduced himself. "Mornin', my name's M. J. Harger. I'm the Warren County deputy." He then turned his attention to the gunshot victim on the floor.

"Hey Stanhope, what the hell happened?" he asked his longtime friend.

Stanhope responded to the deputy's question while reconfirming the identity of the shooter to be Calib McHenry. "Guess, he was after me for gitten' his damn no-good brother. That's the only thing I know, M.J."

At that point, the stage guard offered an explanation for his involvement in the incident, adding that the dead man had been a passenger on the stage that started its run from Saint Louis earlier in the morning. The deputy calmly turned to one of the onlookers standing outside the doorway and issued instructions, "Stanhope's gonna need Doc Clark to care for him later up at his office, but go get Doc now and tell him we need him down here to see Stanhope. Tell Doc he's been shot!"

With some self-assurance, I felt Stanhope was in no mortal danger and believing him to be a lucky fellow, I refrained from introducing myself to the deputy and returned to my seat inside the coach. The mother had successfully quieted her baby who had returned to sleep once again. While the horses were being exchanged gave me time for my lunch and to stretch my legs.

The guard hoisted the outgoing mail sack up to the driver, then climbed aboard and assumed his place on the seat beside his partner. The horse team exchange had taken place during the ordeal and the stage was now ready to roll once again. With the crack of the driver's whip, the newly refreshed hitch team pulled away, and we resumed our Concord run to Columbia.

12

The Civil War had little effect on the city of Columbia's infrastructure. No battles had occurred within the city; however, the nearby communities of Booneville and Centralia were wracked with major battles and conflict.

The area was originally settled in 1806 with the town being founded in 1818 and becoming the county seat of Boone County that year. The original plans for the town had set aside land for Columbia College that was later to become the University of Missouri.

It remained pro-Union during the entire war, primarily due to the heavily garrisoned Union forces encamped there. However, the surrounding Boone County was strongly pro-Confederate as was a great portion of central Missouri. The majority of folks living in the rural areas in this part of the state carried strong sympathy for the Confederate cause and for slavery.

Prior to 1861, all of Boone County and Columbia had benefited from a flourishing economy primarily due to their strategic location on important cross-country routes stretching west to the extent of the frontier. It was an important stagecoach stop on both the Santa Fe and Oregon trails. On any given day, a number of immigrant settlers heading west were likely to make a temporary stop in Columbia for rest, supplies of all kinds, wagon repairs, food, and drink. The oxen and horses accompanying the travelers also had need for food and water that the city could provide. The taverns and other businesses eagerly welcomed the weary travelers and they were prepared to supply whatever their needs might be.

ooooo

After the tragic discovery of Idabel's suicide that early morning, Silas Watson's outlook on life suddenly changed. Now filled with grief and even anger at times, he found it increasingly difficult on some occasions to minister to his patients because of his lasting depression. Nothing seemed of importance to Silas. For a second time, he found himself alone and without a loving wife in his home. The reality of his having already entered the early evening of his life merely accentuated his depressed state of mind.

After Idabel's death, Silas had naturally become even more dependent upon Cele and Lena for encouragement and support. He continued to mark time with little interest or hope for himself or his future. But with time and prayer, the doctor gradually began to acknowledge the seriousness of his mental state and he disliked what he was seeing.

ooooo

One evening when Silas stepped outside his office for some fresh air, a cool breeze was producing an early chill. Hopeful for seeking some companionship and solace from Gracie he approached the mare's stable and found her quietly munching hay.

While affectionately stroking and patting her neck and mane, his eyes welled with tears. Only recently he had begun to ponder the prospect of his leaving Columbia and moving west for a new beginning. But it was this particular evening when he began to have serious thought to such a possibility. He knew it would be very difficult leaving the city with its people he had come to love over the years.

Beginning to sense a tender compassion from his gentle mare, scattered new thoughts began racing through his mind. Perhaps his leaving would erase many of his unpleasant memories and improve him physically and emotionally. Should he remain in Columbia, he might never dismiss the sadness from which he was trying so desperately to escape. A change of his surroundings and the beginning of a fresh new medical practice would likely provide him new energy.

As he continued to pat his faithful friend, this mixture of new thoughts and ideas began to stimulate every impulse throughout his body. Strangely, Silas began to feel energized and appeased by the sudden and welcomed cloud of spiritual comfort that was beginning to settle over him. For the first time in a very long while, Silas began to experience a sense of happiness. As evening darkness engulfed the city, the doctor dropped to his knees in prayer, asking for the Lord's help and guidance.

After Silas returned to the house, the stimulating new thoughts continued. Most important to Silas was the fact that all were happy thoughts. He was convinced there was still much happiness for him to experience during the remaining years of his life.

Out of the blue, he was reminded of his having made an offer to his young nephew for a partnership in practice. Perhaps the young man was already on his journey to Columbia. If that were so, perhaps Somers would be interested in merely taking over his busy practice.

Silas picked up the small oil lamp from his desk and made his way upstairs to bed already confident this was going to be a night when he would finally have a restful sleep. He could not remember when he'd last had that experience.

ooooo

While preparing the doctor's breakfast, a loud knock on the front parlor door caught Lena's attention. She hurried there and when opening the door was confronted by a nondescript heavyset lady visibly shaking and excitedly wringing her hands. Lena was unsure of her name but was quite certain the lady was Birdie Henshaw's neighbor.

"Birdie's havin' bad labor pains and is about to have her baby. She needs Doc right away," the excited woman cried out.

Silas calmly made his appearance at the doorway and said, "Tell Birdie I'll be right there." He hoped his relaxed manner might give Birdie's neighbor some assurance and help dispel her concern.

"Thank you, Doc. I'll run and tell her right away," the lady answered already showing more restraint. She faced around and carried on up the street with the doctor's message.

"Save my breakfast, Lena. It's doubtful this should take long; I should be back soon," the doctor chided. After retrieving his grip, he hurried out the door to deliver Birdie's baby. After a restful night's sleep, the new day had already become more blessed and happier for Dr. Silas Watson.

ooooo

Now that I think about it, as our stagecoach drew nearer to the Concordia home station in Columbia, I was feeling both excitement and some apprehension. When stepping down from the stage, I noticed a young livery boy standing idly beside his wagon-hitch. I called out to him asking if he would fetch my trunk from the coach and then render me to my destination.

After rearranging the other luggage and cargo, the guard had my trunk moved from atop the coach and onto the boy's wagon. The boy assured me he was familiar with Dr. Watson's office location, and we departed. After a short ride through town, the boy brought his wagon to a stop in front of my uncle's office and home.

I was immediately taken with the handsome two-story dwelling and surrounding property. After moving my trunk to the front steps, I thanked the boy and paid his fee. He gave thanks and after jumping onto his wagon, quickly disappeared down the street.

I entered onto the veranda and rapped on the office door several times but without response. I assumed Uncle Silas was either on a home call or taking a well-deserved early afternoon nap. I settled myself down on the step and rested myself against the old trunk to await the doctor's presence.

Although weary, I felt good having the long trip behind me. It proved far more eventful and tiring than I had anticipated. After closing my eyes and having a few moments of reflection, my thoughts returned to Liz. I found myself pondering if she was happy and settled comfortably with her new family and work.

ooooo

While Silas was casually walking back to his office, he continued to hum a favorite tune and mused about the Henshaw baby boy he had just delivered. He had to admit the big boy certainly had a healthy cry. With his grip in one hand, Silas was returning home with a flour sack in the other. It was filled with fresh garden vegetables along with some of Birdie's delicious bread and preserves. He had been given the sack's contents for partial payment for his service in the delivery. He always appreciated such thoughtful generosity from his patients when they were without sufficient money to pay for the entire sum of his services.

As he sauntered down the street lost in reverie, his once troubled mind was beginning to find peace. With the difficult decision now having been made, he must begin making plans for his move. After so many years in Columbia, bidding his patients and friends a final good-bye was going to be very difficult. Silas was certain he must begin preparing himself for it.

When he arrived at the gate of the decorative fence surrounding his property, he was bewildered when noting a man apparently asleep on his veranda. Approaching closer and then noting the large brown trunk, Silas knew it had to be his nephew. Pausing for a moment then making a closer examination, the old doctor found it hard to believe the changes in the young man since last seeing him as a small rambunctious boy. Silas chuckled to himself while noting one thing to be certain, the young man's facial features certainly did not belie whom his cantankerous father might be. Silas found it hard to believe his nephew, now a physician, had arrived in Columbia to join him in practice. Excitedly, he set down his grip and sack on the step and tapped lightly on his nephew's shoulder.

"Somers, my boy, welcome to my home and to Columbia. I'm so glad you've arrived safe from harm's way."

I was aroused and bemused when hearing the mention of my name. "Uncle Silas! With God's providence I made it! Apart from being a little spent, I'm so glad to be here. It's been so long since I've seen you."

Then with a wide grin on his face, Silas joked, "Let's get you moved inside. Some patient may think I've got a dead one on my veranda! I'll have Cele move your trunk upstairs. Lena will get you settled in one of the spare bedrooms. Do you need something to eat? They must be out back in their quarters and didn't hear your knock."

Once inside, Silas commanded loudly, "We need help out here. Cele, come quickly!"

I could tell my arrival had created both excitement and impatience for my uncle. It was quite evident in his voice. Then turning and facing me and now with a serious but more natural voice he explained, "Cele and Lena have been with me for years. I'll acquaint you with them. You're probably not accustomed as to how we get things done out here. You need not ask, just tell 'em. It will be no trouble to you, for whatever you want done, they'll do it for you.."

Cele and Lena promptly presented themselves before us in the parlor room. Silas made the introductions of the new house resident and gave explicit instructions for getting me settled in.

Silas then turned, saying, "After Lena gets you settled in your upstairs room, at your leisure, come down so you might view our office. We must get caught up on everything. Damn, it's good to have you come to join me!"

My uncle's unaffected demeanor and elation provided me with a warm feeling. I shared the same sentiments for him. I was now self-assured that a new chapter in my life was about to begin.

Over the following days, my uncle and I became reacquainted and began sharing many personal experiences and thoughts. I learned of his marriage to Idabel and of her recent death. In our conversations, it was evident what an effect her death had on him.

I must admit I was eager to learn about his war experiences, which he eventually began to share. Several days passed before he began relating about his unrelenting grief and mental depression that had developed following Idabel's death. He shared his reasons and what preliminary plans he had in mind for leaving town.

I was caught totally unawares and had some trepidation when hearing of his plans for leaving, but I could understand. When he put the question to me if I would be interested in adopting his medical practice, I was greatly honored and excited, but also bewildered.

Doubtless, there would be favor for my assuming his practice; however, his other proposal for a joint adventure moving further out onto the expanding frontier promised to be even more challenging and auspicious to me. Be that as it may, many questions began to lay heavily on my mind since I had never anticipated being confronted with such a decision so early in my professional career.

ooooo

Because of his great reluctance in leaving Columbia and especially his patients, Uncle Silas and I continued with our joint practice in Columbia for just over two years after my arrival. I came to enjoy the city which I discovered so different from Philadelphia. I was enjoying my work and had learned so much from my uncle.

Nevertheless, my uncle continued making preparations and reconfirmed his earlier decision for leaving. I remained torn with my decision whether or not to accompany him. During our time together, we had grown so close. His kind, gentle manner was providing me a father I had never known, and in addition, an excellent teacher of medicine.

My real education came from observing how he treated each of his patients' illnesses and injuries, and more important how he treated each of them as human beings. That became an important issue for me. I gave great value to his advice and his helpful criticism. While in medical school, I was never exposed to the practical knowledge and wisdom he was sharing. I also had begun to realize how much self-confidence I was gaining with my personal treatment of patients.

Yes, I had been an honor graduate of a distinguished medical school, but that was all behind me and in reality meant nothing. While in Columbia, I learned what mattered most and that was gaining experience. I had found a great teacher. After much careful and prayerful thought, I brought myself to a decision.

13

In the early fall of 1867, loaded with our medical equipment, supplies, and personal belongings, Silas and I boarded a train that would take us and our cargo further west in Missouri to a town called Sedalia. By that time, Sedalia had already become a growing frontier community while serving as a strategic railhead during the war years. By 1867 with the rail expansion and new construction, the town was not only becoming a greater rail hub but was also becoming a cattle town. With growing demand for beef in the north and east, cattle drives into Sedalia's stockyards had become important and more frequent prior to their shipment elsewhere by train. We believed the town would be a good location for our new practice.

War's influence on Sedalia, Missouri, was similar to other towns in the state. New construction and business growth was dependent, at times, on what influence the persistent fear of guerrilla warfare was having on arriving immigrants, both in town and the surrounding area. While this relentless fear drove some folks away, others remained and to their eventual benefit. However, there were times when bloody and sometimes deadly skirmishes took place on the town's streets. Sedalia's dedicated and stubborn residents found that carrying a personal weapon for protection was necessary.

Fortunately, during those troubled years, several brave and optimistic merchants remained steadfast. Their tenacity eventually brought further prosperity but with that prosperity also came inherent problems. In 1864, Sedalia was finally chosen the county seat for Pettis County only after considerable political upheaval. However, once it had been chosen for the county's center of government, confidence in the town and business was significantly renewed. By 1866, Sedalia had gained not only several dry goods and mercantile businesses, but hardware stores, blacksmith shops, churches, and more than one druggist. During that busy year, Sedalia was witnessing the construction of its first bank; a very important and good sign.

With the town's location just ninety miles east of Kansas City, 190 miles west from Saint Louis, and the important Missouri River being only thirty miles distant, Sedalia received protection from an established Union military post that remained active until its closure in 1865. Despite the nearby Union's detachment for protection, infrequent but dangerous Confederate raids in the surrounding Pettis County area brought unrelenting fear for many of the town's residents.

A brief yet tragic crisis occurred in the fall of 1864. Confederate invaders were able to overpower the Union militia post. They began to ravage and despoil the town with senseless abandon. With destruction and chaos raining down, for reasons never to be made known and for the town's good fortune, a Confederate general arrived. He immediately put down his troop's senseless destruction and looting. Whatever the general's motive might have been that day, he ordered all of his spiteful comrades out of town. Thanks to that sane general, Sedalia was returned into the Union's hands for its protection thereafter.

ooooo

Following our uneventful journey on the train to Sedalia, we discovered a livery stable near the railroad depot with a pen of horses that were for sale. We made our way directly to the pen so that

Uncle Silas might inspect each of them. He made his way over the fence and began looking closely at each one. For a city boy like me, I found it interesting and educational while watching him. After our purchase of two horses, a buggy and a flat bed four-wheel hitch wagon, we set out to find temporary living quarters in some boarding house.

Silas drove the buggy while I followed in the buckboard now loaded with our belongings. Being unfamiliar with our new surroundings, we slowly made our way along what appeared to be a main road through town. We later learned it was Ohio Street. We shared interest in seeing several large two-story structures constructed of both wood and brick. Noting the variety of merchants already established in town, each appeared prosperous with a number of the town's residents milling around on the street. We felt assured Sedalia would continue to grow and we would become part of that growth.

I perused the new surroundings with great anticipation. As we continued our slow journey along south Ohio Street, we passed the First National Bank, an obviously new brick building with an elegant appearance. Along the way we also observed the early construction of a building that was destined to become the Sedalia Opera House and another that would later become the new Methodist Church.

Although I could appreciate evidence of early social and cultural refinement, I also visualized a community with rough edges that would be certain to make our lives interesting in the future. Be that as it may, I was excited to have arrived with my uncle and was confident there would be many challenges ahead for Sedalia's two newest doctors.

After traveling some distance from the livery stable, we stopped outside a well-attended two-story building. Our attention was drawn first to a large sign above its entry that read, "The Independent Press." We naturally assumed it to be the local newspaper office and a likely place for having our questions answered. We tied our horses on the rail and entered the building.

We received a friendly greeting from a short stubby gentleman fitted out with a long soiled apron over his blouse and trousers. I was immediately taken by the unforgiving, pungent odor of ink that was permeating the office. We presumed the gentleman greeting us was the likely editor. I noticed he was wearing tiny wire-framed eyeglasses with extra-thick lens. He was bald with the exception of heavy gray locks of hair partially hiding each ear.

"Good day, gentlemen. What can Charlie Webster do for you this fine day?"

"We've just arrived in these parts, and we're in search of a clean boarding house. My name is Silas Watson, and this is my nephew and partner, Somers Watson. We've just arrived in town and have made plans to begin a joint medical practice here in Sedalia."

"Well, praise our God Almighty! Our prayers have been answered! Welcome to Sedalia, Doctors! My name is Charlie Webster, and I am guilty of being *The Democrat*'s editor. Around town, I just go by Charlie, and folks either love or hate me. By now, I've learned I simply can't please 'em all. I know a downright comfortable place for you to find rooms, but what's more important—do ya have a place for your office?"

"We just came in on the train, so we can use any advice or help you or your fellow merchants might offer," I added. We were happy to see the editor's enthusiasm and thankful for his cordial welcome.

"I'd be most happy to help ya, gentlemen. Doctors, please do come back to my office so we can talk, and I'll see what we can get done for Sedalia's new doctors." Charlie ushered us through a room containing a large printing press and crowded with stacked rolls of newsprint. We finally made our way to his small office at a rear corner of the building.

Charlie's small cramped and cluttered office space was lined with several tall stacks of bundled outdated and obviously unread newspapers. Scores of newspaper clippings, papers, and notes with scribbled messages littered the top of his roll-top desk and the floor beneath.

"Gentlemen, please give pardon to my small office and please take a seat. I know my office hain't the best for bein' organized, but you can bet a five-dollar gold piece I still know where I can find everything when the need comes my way."

Now looking more serious, Charlie began, "Doctors, as both of you may already know, we're a mighty new community. Sedalia first 'came a town only four year ago with a population of only 300 folks, but just last year we numbered 1,500 and still growin'.

"The Union forces were fortified out on the edge of town during the war to protect our great railroads. However, the government has jus' recently shut down the fort. Now that our railroads have continued growin' and the cattle drives from down in Texas have recently begun comin' our way, all this is bringin' new prosperity to our little town as you'll see.

With all the incomin' folks workin' on the railroads and Texas cow drovers by the hundreds comin' through town every few days, business has been damn good. Wagon after wagon full of settlers are comin' and homesteadin' farm acres in all directions from town. 'Coarse we also have those good-for-nothin' vagrants passin' through that stir things up on occasion.

However, Doctors, I must warn you that with all these men folks arrivin', the town has begun to get overrun with public women or whores as I always call 'em." With a chuckle and wry grin on his face, he continued, "A few new ones arrive each week or two. Apparently, they also find business good. Then with a wink he added, "Yah, we've got our share of vice, but we tend to overlook all that womanly business since their madam's monthly fines do add to our town's treasury.

You'll note several new buildings under construction and some new dwellins' in different areas of town. By the way, we've got some druggists in town that should be of great help to you. So I think you'll be impressed with our commendable business district."

We continued listening intently to Charlie's story, all of which was helpful and entertaining. With his description of the business and social changes taking place, I was certain Sedalia had great opportunity for continued growth, and his story only reconfirmed for each of us that real challenges lay ahead.

ooooo

Thanks to Charlie Webster and several of his business friends, over the following few days we were fortunate in locating a large two-story dwelling on south Ohio Street. Its ideal location was in the direction where the growing business area was extending. The dwelling was quite similar to the one Silas had owned in Columbia.

By chance, the handsome property only happened to be for sale because its elderly owner had recently lost his life in a run away buggy crash outside town. The old gentleman was well known in the community and had been one of Sedalia's earliest businessmen who had retained his optimism for the developing community and refused to leave. In fact, time and again he would boast that he would take death before any scoundrel would drive him from town.

Our newly purchased property had a somewhat larger ground floor for our office than in Columbia. Spacious living quarters were available for us once again on the second floor. Like the house in Columbia a small room for maid's quarters was located near the kitchen at the rear of the house. A large stable and attached buggy shed were located in the back that was to be shared with a neighbor. A separate small building adjoining the stable had apparently been used for slave quarters at one time.

After nearly two weeks working long hours each day, Uncle Silas and I were finally comfortably settled and prepared to open our new office. Charlie Webster was kind enough to make mention of our new practice of medicine in his newspaper on more than one occasion. It was an exciting and enjoyable new experience for me. We were pleased with our location, but now we were in need of caretakers with the likes of Cele and Lena. They had chosen to remain in Columbia with other members of their family.

14

We enjoyed a very successful first year in Sedalia. During that year another doctor moved into town and our community continued its growth as we had expected. It was customary, especially on days of good weather, to see the streets crowded with country folks with their wagons loaded with supplies in preparation for their return home.

Several one and two-story buildings were constructed for housing new businesses along with several private homes. The Methodist Church was completed, as was the Opera House. Land for several miles each direction from town continued to draw new immigrant homesteaders.

As before, we found some folks arriving with little money and unable to pay for our services. Most paid with what money they could on their bill and supplemented it with a variety of foodstuffs they had prepared or raised in their gardens. However, unlike Columbia, there were more transients in Sedalia and many left town with our bills unpaid and were never seen or heard from again.

We were pleased with the professional relationship we were sharing with the residents in our new community. A major problem we continued to face, as everywhere, was the limited number of quality medicines available for our use. Quite often we had nothing more than compassion and words of encouragement for our patients and their family members. We were often called upon to simply recommend the use of time-proven home remedies.

During my brief time in medicine, I had already learned an important lesson. Whether my patient's health problem improved and he got well, or if it should worsen and he should die, had little bearing on any special skill or knowledge I might have. The final outcome depended on God's will. This was an important but difficult lesson for me to learn.

Our early experiences in Sedalia rekindled in our minds what old Charlie Webster foretold that first day in his office—our town would not only grow in size and numbers but also become increasingly raucous and rough with corruption and vice. Charlie's prediction could not have been more accurate!

ooooo

A prolonged deluge of rain had fallen in our area for the better part of two days. When the temperature dropped each night, the rain changed into sleet and snow. That combination created miserable conditions both on the dirt streets in town and on the country roads.

It was my night to be on call. As the day's weather had progressively deteriorated, I held out hope that I would not be called on to treat some drunken rail worker or cowboy after their having been shot in one of the saloons over some argument or unpaid gambling debt. I learned early that such events were not uncommon in Sedalia.

James Crafton, wearing only a light cotton coat, stood shivering on our dark veranda. Throughout the early evening hours, the temperature had continued to drop. After Mr. Crafton had made several frantic blows on the door, our housekeeper responded to his knock and was confronted by the anxious young man.

Lottie held the door open for the gentleman and commanded, "Lawzy, lawzy, mister. What you need? Come in here right now an' warm yourself, my child."

"It's my wife. She needs the doctor. Seems she jus' can't get that baby out. Our helper's been with her all the time, but she can't get it done. Will ya tell the doctor?" James pleaded in desperation.

I overheard some of their conversation and hurried to the door. I recognized the young man to be James Crafton.

'It's my missus, Doc. The baby just won't come. Please come out to the house." James's desperation was clearly evident as he continued massaging together his cold bare hands.

"I'll get my buggy"—but James interrupted me.

"Don't never mind, Doc. I'll fetch you out there on my buckboard. The rain and snow's got us some really deep mud, but my Baby Joe will pull us through." I didn't dispute his word, and we left shortly for James's farm nearly four miles west of town.

James was correct. The going was difficult and I was convinced my buggy-hitch would have been no count with those conditions. Baby Joe, the Crafton's large ox, slowly but safely, pulled the heavy wagon through several deep ruts and across two swollen creeks, each out of their banks with a torrent of icy cold water. As we approached the Crafton cabin, it appeared to be dark except for a dim light coming from a rear window. It was late evening. I did note the pleasant smell of burning wood rising from the cabin's chimney.

James quickly ushered me inside where the fireplace contained a roaring fire that was partially illuminating the cabin's interior. From behind a draw curtain that cordoned off a back corner of the cabin, I could hear moans and whimpering. I hurried to the expectant mother's bedside and bid her a good evening. The short stocky and elderly midwife's face displayed helpless anxiety as she continued to wipe perspiration from her patient's forehead.

"My missus jus' can't push the baby out. I needs yur help, Doctor. We've been tryin' for a long time now, but I can't help her no more." There was total frustration in the woman's voice; however she did appear somewhat relieved with my presence at the bedside.

After removing my heavy wet coat, I too welcomed the warmth coming from the roaring fire. As I began to roll up the sleeves on my blouse, I requested she fetch a clean bed sheet and pitcher of warm water. Turning my attention to Mrs. Crafton, she also gave me every indication of being fretful and quite exhausted.

I gently placed my partially warmed hands upon her swollen belly and a few moments later, I could feel it become rock-hard. Without question, Mrs. Crafton was in labor and appeared to be having strong uterine contractions. After a careful examination of the young mother, I could find no unusual problems. When listening to the baby's heartbeat, I believed it also to be normal. Slowly moving my hands across her abdomen once again, I could detect the baby's movements inside her womb. From all indications mother and baby were doing well. With the aide of some pain medication to help her relax, I felt certain we would have a healthy baby in a reasonably short time.

"Mrs. Crafton, I'll give you a little medicine that will make you feel much better. After you get relaxed, we should be able to have your baby. What names have you picked out?" I was hoping to detract her thoughts and dispel some of her anxiety.

"If it's a boy, he'll be named James Junior or Elsibeth if it's a girl. I know it's a terribly bad night outside. Thank you, Doctor, for comin'," she answered with relief already registered in her voice as she wiped away tears from her eyes and cheeks.

"I administered a small quantity of Laudanum, and in a brief time, I could see my patient beginning to relax. The midwife hurried away to fetch some cloth towels and a pitcher of water from the large iron caldron hanging over the fire.

Later that hour, the loud piercing cry from a baby boy filled the cabin to the relief and joy of everyone. Mrs. Crafton fell to weeping with delight when I placed her firstborn to her swollen breast. Following a tender parting handshake with the new mother, I gathered together my instruments and supplies and reached for my coat.

James had already removed two heavy quilts and a buffalo robe from a nearby cupboard in preparation for our return trip to town. We found Baby Joe patiently waiting where James had tied him earlier near the front gate, but now the ox's dark red coat was covered with a thick layer of ice and heavy wet snow.

Snow continued falling as James and I made our slow journey back to town. The wagon's lanterns helped reveal portions of the deep ruts in the road we had previously navigated. By now they had become nearly filled once again with snow. The return trip was considerably more relaxing for us. The joyful new father and I carried on a continuous conversation while Baby Joe pulled our wagon slowly through the deepening mud and snow.

Well after the midnight hour, we arrived in town, and shortly thereafter, I fell into my warm bed. It had been an anxious night for me, but all had gone well.

ooooo

"How was your night, Somers?" Silas inquired the following morning over breakfast.

"The delivery went fine. Got a healthy big boy for the Crafton's, but the trip out and back was cold and miserable." Then I added in jest, "By the way, I hope you enjoyed your warm bed while I was out plowing through that mud and snow!"

After stroking his white beard several times, a broad mischievous smile crossed his face, and he responded to my sarcastic remark, "Chalk that one up to experience my good man."

Walking into our office following his breakfast, my uncle was surprised to find two men of young age seated on the waiting room bench. They were disheveled with trousers and high-topped boots covered with dried mud. Both men had spurs attached to their boots. Their appearance alone told the doctor they were cattle drovers, yet Silas deemed it most unusual for drovers to be arriving in town with cattle so late in the season in light of the bad weather conditions of late.

With a voice filled with excitement and anger, one drover explained, "Doc, my frien' David got stuck in his side last night with a knife. We were jus' havin' a drink and mindin' our own business when that damn bushwacker guy started pickin' a fight. Lo an' behold, he pulled a knife and jabbed it right into David's side, then the coward took off. The bar man hurried and put this ban'age on him. David needs some help an' then we're goin' after that bastard. We'll get him!"

Silas ushered the silent but injured drover into the exam room where he removed a soiled and blood-soaked wadding of cloth covering the wound. He discovered an open two-inch shallow wound immediately above the man's left hipbone. From his preliminary examination, Silas was doubtful that vital organs were involved in light of the wound's location and depth.

"This may be a bit painful, my boy. But I've gotta clean it up and get it closed for ya," Silas warned. The cowboy offered no response.

Silas proceeded to carefully wipe and clean the wound of dried blood. After repeated cleansing of the wound with alcohol, he examined it closely for any other debris. The cut from the assailant's knife blade had produced a wound with smooth edges. Using cotton thread, Silas closed the wound. Before applying a clean dressing and roller bandage, he poured an ample quantity of alcohol over the repaired wound.

"You're a very lucky young man, my friend. Should you get the fever with this in the next day or so it would mean you've likely got an infection. Listen to me, cowboy. Infection can kill you, so watch for it. If you get along and are still around, see me in a few days."

The cowboys handed over what money they had left from the previous night's visit in the saloon and quickly left the office. Silas sat down at his desk and began perusing Charlie's newspaper from the previous day. It was time for him to get caught up on the latest tell tales around town.

15

After the close of the war and closely linked with the great expansion of the rail system, many transient workers sought employment for its construction. As one might expect, Sedalia had its share of those workers, many of dubious character. They were often seen milling along the town's streets and frequently found drunk and belligerent inside the local saloons and other places around town. With the start of frequent trail drives coming into town transient cowboy drovers, many in their teens, added to the problem. These rough adventuresome young men, after weeks of loneliness on the trail, were more than anxious to be entertained by whatever manner the town might have to offer.

With all of these transients coming and going through town each day, another quite different group began arriving but chose to remain permanent in Sedalia. They were the "public women or whores," as most of the locals referred to them.

Prostitution prospered and continued to grow like other businesses in town. These women, of varying age, arrived and proved to be well versed as to where and how to begin their new business.

A number of Sedalia's upstanding and astute business merchants were quick to acknowledge the needs of this rapidly growing new group of town residents. The women of the night were a sure bet on becoming renters for various properties the merchant's might own. Typically, a respectable and general mercantile business occupied the ground floor with a brothel or "social house" rental on the second. Several of the town's popular brothels sprang up within a short distance from the tracks of the Missouri–Pacific railroad.

Prostitution in Sedalia had been proclaimed illegal by a city ordinance. The newspaper's publisher and the town's clergy had also condemned it. However, ambivalence arose and with time, reigned supreme. The astute town fathers realized their town's treasury had begun to grow and was even showing a profit from the new female arrivals in town. A portion of that new income was coming from weekly and monthly fines levied on the madams and their ladies. And what's more, general business was increasing and much appreciated by shop owners and landlords. And of added interest was the fact that all those ladies also happened to be consumers for all types of goods being sold in the merchants' shops.

For these many reasons, ambivalence seemed worthy and remained quietly acceptable with most merchants. Whether it was prostitution, gambling, alcohol, or other vices, the increased migration of people into Sedalia and surrounding area was creating a prosperous yet unsettled frontier community that would eventually require several years to become more dignified and refined.

Thaddeus Moore was such a businessman and might well have received the epithet of *entrepreneur*. He had originally come to Sedalia from Maryland where he had owned and operated a very profitable furniture and cabinet business. His craftsmanship with wood was of high repute along the east coast. With knowledge of the great number of immigrants heading to the new frontier, he recognized a new business opportunity. And like many, Thaddeus shared the immigrants' spirit and enthusiasm for adventure, but foremost, he enjoyed making money!

Moore arrived in tiny Sedalia in the early spring of 1860 with its population numbering less than 300 and only a short time after the community had been officially sanctioned to become a city. With a fair sum of personal money brought from Maryland, Mr. Moore made plans for construction of a spacious two-story wood building on property he had purchased facing Ohio Street and but a short distance from Sixth Street. It was in that building where he planned to establish his new cabinet and furniture manufacturing business. His specifications called for the wood shop to be housed on the ground floor while his personal living quarters would occupy the large second floor.

Moore's Cabinet and Furniture Store, as it was known, became successful quickly. Many new settlers and some established town merchants all needed furniture and Moore became the man to see. Ironically during his first year in business, his talented craftsmanship was requested occasionally by some of the more wealthy families to construct a coffin for one of their deceased members. His coffin business began to grow just like his furniture business. Thaddeus recognized that his newest business was becoming a distinctive and ideal complement to his furniture business.

The population of Sedalia had increased 50 percent by the year 1866. By that time, the city included a growing number of buildings that housed a variety of businesses from banking to blacksmiths and saloons. There were three churches, three grocery stores, several hardware and dry goods stores, and more than one druggist that had made their appearance in the community.

With his furniture and coffin business a success, an entirely new and profitable idea came to mind for the enterprising Mr. Moore. He reasoned that if he could provide the coffin, why not provide the first and only undertaker and funeral service. Without pause, he taught himself the art and technique of embalming a corpse, and in a short time, another new business was introduced into the prospering town.

After his purchase of a preexisting but smaller building next door, Thaddeus moved his funeral business into the newly purchased building with his handcrafted coffins on permanent public display in a room at the rear of the small building. By design, the display room had direct access off a narrow alley that soon gained the moniker "Coffin Alley." By using the alley entrance, the bereaved family members were permitted privacy while making their selection of a coffin. As one might expect, each of Thaddeus Moore's new businesses continued to thrive.

Mr. Moore's good fortune continued when perchance in the fall of 1866 he found, and soon after married, the first and only true love of his life. She was the pretty and vivacious Ruthie Grayson from Kansas City. Ruthie had become a young war widow when her Union officer husband lost his life in the Battle of Carthage in Jasper County in July 1861. Ruthie proved to be very much like her newly wed but elder husband. She possessed not just a desire for making money, but a talent!

By their mutually contrived, eccentric and unorthodox plan, Ruthie was to become the madam for an elegant brothel that the newly married couple planned to create on the furniture store's second floor. The first order of business in Ruthie's carefully scrutinized plan called for a complete remodel of the current second floor area. It was planned that two small apartments would be constructed at the front of the building. They would share a private covered stairway to the front rising off Ohio Street. Each apartment would be rented to an upstanding married couple.

The remaining floor space design would call for a short central hallway with access to four small bedrooms—two on opposite sides of the hall. A small but opulent well-appointed parlor at the rear of the building would have access to the hallway and bedrooms. A very small private kitchen would adjoin the parlor in the back. An outside stairway with private entrance leading from Coffin Alley would provide direct access to the parlor. That back stairway would permit privacy creme de la creme for Ruthie's clients. To complete her decorative plan, an elaborate ceramic washbasin and large pitcher would sit atop one of her husband's masterly crafted washstands in one corner of each bedroom with its matching ceramic chamber pot at side.

The Moore's plan called for each bedroom to be rented to a lady of the upper class stratum both in physical appearance and demeanor. The four ladies would be carefully screened and selected from all applicants by Mrs. Moore. Each chosen woman would be required to pay a monthly bed fee for her assigned room. In addition, she would be required to pay the madam a pre-arranged fee based on her monthly business.

Known as Ruthie's House, the swank bordello became an instant success. Ruthie's carefully selected ladies began servicing a steady stream of "qualified men of financial means" from off the back alley. Madam Ruthie, as full-time owner and manager, paid close attention to all clients coming and going and to the fees being generated by each of her elegant ladies.

Each year on Christmas Eve, Thaddeus made certain that his close personal friend, who just happened to be the city marshal, always received his annual Christmas envelope. The special envelope always contained a generous sum of money so as to provide assurance that the Coffin Alley door to Ruthie's business would always remain open year-round "without needless harassment, interruption, or unnecessary city fines." Several businesses followed Thaddeus and Ruthie Moore's penchant for making money through prostitution, yet none could ever equal the class of Ruthie's House.

ooooo

Moses Kimbrough, by his very nature, was another unique character that ventured into town one sunny day. The new visitor arrived in his mule-drawn wagon while sharing its seat with his business partner who was probably even more unusual than Moses. On the bed of the wagon were several unopened boxes, each containing twelve tall bottles of Kimbrough's Magic Elixir. The potent mixture was personally manufactured and bottled by Moses himself.

A large wooden sign attached to each side of the wagon read:

Pastor Moses Kimbrough
Faith Healer and Prophet

While slowly rolling along down East Broadway Street, the wagon with its two occupants captured the curious glances and comments from town folks milling about on the street. By his very nature, the pastor's physical appearance and stature drew those quizzical glances. A massive snow-white beard with long drooping mustache reached well below mid chest. A crumpled and soiled clerical collar, at one time probably white in color, circled his neck and was attached to his gray broad cloth blouse. His waistcoat and soiled dusty black outer coat and trousers gave evidence of the man's obvious number of miles and weeks spent traveling dusty roads.

The pastor's partner was much younger in years with his face showing a persistent timid but mousey expression. By habit, his tiny spectacles rested low on his nose. The slender wimpy-appearing man's business dress consisted of a faded plaid blouse with soiled gray trousers secured in place by a pair of wide leather braces. His trouser bottoms were bunched into the tops of tall military boots. An ill-fitting, dusty, and sweat-stained bowler with wide crown rested squarely atop his head.

Upon observing one of Sedalia's popular saloons on the corner of Broadway and Osage streets, the pastor brought the wagon slowly to a halt a short distance from the entrance. After handing over the reins to his assistant, Pastor Kimbrough raised his tall frame up from the seat and jumped down from the buckboard.

After a quick dusting of his coat sleeves, Moses uttered confidently to his partner, "I'll go in and stir the place up with a little religion. I'm sure they all need it. You wait here. I'll fetch a big crowd of sinners out here before you know it."

Moses then stood ramrod tall and straight, readjusted the lapels on his soiled coat, and squared his shoulders. He approached the saloon's entrance, pushed the wooden free-swinging doors inward, and marched undaunted into the noisy and smoke-filled premises. Pastor Kimbrough was on a mission. Once inside and with a thundering voice, he shouted, "God is watching you, sinners! I am his prophet, and I have traveled day and night to finally arrive here to save each and every last one of you from hell! Yes folks, I said from hell!"

A hush fell across the large crowded room with all eyes turned toward the tall older gentleman standing inside the doorway. Having captured their attention, he continued, "My name is Pastor Moses Kimbrough. God has chosen me for the task of healing whatever your sickness or ills may be—yes, even your troubled mind, if necessary. Follow me outside to my wagon, and I'll show you what I mean. You'll be forever grateful. Come now, all of you! My God-given power and special elixir can save each one of you wretched souls."

With that introduction and sermonette, Kimbrough turned and retreated toward his buckboard. Several patrons followed close behind. Their state of drunkenness became quite clear when watching their gait while each person made the short journey out to Kimbrough's wagon. Moments later, another curious group left their seats at the poker tables and made their way outside into the warm bright afternoon sun.

Moses quickly climbed aboard his wagon and elevated himself up onto his buckboard seat. He assumed once again his tall ramrod stance so all could see and hear. Gradually, other inquisitive passersby gathered around the wagon with quizzical expressions on each of their faces. Noting the ever-growing crowd including some women with children, with a booming voice the pastor began his chatter.

"Praise the Lord on high! By your very own volition, you have followed me on this glorious day outside that dungeon of hell to be saved! I praise each of you in so doing. While my assistant passes among you, please make your most generous donation for supporting my ministry and healing as we travel across this broad land. For any of you nonbelievers, let me tell you something. Brother Horace, my assistant, was once blind following an accident when he was but a child of five. Just one year ago he came to me asking for my healing powers. Today, his vision is far better than either yours or mine. Praise the Lord!"

On cue, Brother Horace proudly raised his dusty bowler high into the air, after which he returned it to his head as before. He began circulating through the crowd for their donations.

"Sir, that man out there I'm pointing to that's wearing the black hat and has a kerchief in red; I saw that you appear to have a problem with your wrist. Come up here and tell us about it, my friend."

The young, slight of build trail drover was bemused and embarrassed being singled out from the gathering crowd. Slowly, he scrutinized the crowd standing around him. Finally, he replied with a voice barely audible, "Busted my wrist ropin' one of those crazy damn steers."

Moses shouted, "Come here, my friend, and permit me to heal that arm of yours!"

With great reluctance but cajoled by his equally drunk friends, the cowboy staggered forward from the crowd of onlookers and rested his weight against the wagon. His face was crimson and displayed his inability to fathom what might follow.

The daunting pastor commanded loudly for everyone to hear, "My good man, jump up here with me so all can see what is about to happen. This poor man says he has a broken bone, and I am about to heal him better than he was before that old cow got to him!"

With great effort, the cowboy climbed aboard the wagon. As he took his position next to the pastor, Brother Horace helped steady the weaving and drunken young man.

"Heal this wrist *now!*" Moses shouted while at the same time placing a viselike grip of his large hand around the ignorant young man's swollen and painful wrist. Cringing with pain, the cowboy nearly dropped down to his knees.

"Now, my friend, rub this liniment on twice a day until it's gone and drink every drop of my special elixir from this bottle. Your wrist is healed, my dear friend," Kimbrough commanded.

The cowboy accepted the small tin of liniment and bottle handed to him and climbed down off the wagon. His drover friends assisted him as they made their way back toward the saloon's entrance. Several individuals stepped forward and waved their money to purchase a bottle of Kimbrough's magic elixir out of the freshly opened boxes.

By the following day, Pastor Kimbrough made a decision that he and Brother Horace should remain in Sedalia a few days and make "some real money." They shared a room in a boarding house, and Pastor Moses had already made plans to discover what the town had to offer.

While Kimbrough was engaged in receiving some "very personal gratification" one afternoon, Brother Horace commandeered the wagon with its cargo of elixir and liniment and absconded from town in a cloud of dust with no thought of returning. Moses's afternoon of ecstasy proved far more expensive than he had planned. Dejected, Pastor Kimbrough was last seen boarding the train the following morning headed for Kansas City.

16

"Get him to my office quickly. I've done all I can here," Uncle Silas shouted to the two excited cattle drovers standing nearby. A severely injured black boy of seventeen or eighteen years was lying on the ground inside a cattle pen. With eyes closed, his facial grimace gave witness to his severe pain and shock.

Quincy Wade and fellow cattle drovers of the renowned John Blocker outfit arrived earlier that morning at the railhead with their nearly 1,200 head of longhorns. Shortly after their arrival, the drovers began sorting the herd into smaller groups and moving them into separate pens for later shipment to Chicago by train.

Quincy was the only black drover in Blocker's outfit for that drive. He was well liked by everyone. During the sorting process, the handsome black drover was pushed backward and pinned against one of the pen's tall wooden gates by several animals. Before the lad could free himself, a steer violently gored the drover in his lower abdomen.

Heeding the doctor's abrupt command, the two excited drovers ran from the pen to locate a wagon-hitch for transporting the lad. Shortly after, the two excited drovers returned with a wagon and were now joined by two volunteer drovers who had come along to assist in moving Quincy to the doctor's office. After the boy's injured body was gently placed onto the wagon, Silas grabbed the horse's reins and with the four anxious drovers swiftly left the yards and headed down the street to his office.

Following their arrival, Quincy was immediately given an extra large dose of morphine. It was followed by Silas's meticulous examination of the gravely injured young man lying on the porcelain table. As expected, he found the wound severely contaminated with various pieces and fibers of cloth, dirt, dried blood and considerable foul smelling muck from the cattle pen's muddy floor. After quickly cleaning away as much of the debris as possible to permit a more detailed examination, he regretfully discovered what he had feared most. The animal's horn had penetrated deeply into the boy's lower body cavity and had produced a small but open puncture wound in the bowel. Greenish colored bowel contents could be seen spilling freely into the boy's abdominal cavity. The old surgeon's war experience had taught him that penetrating wounds like this were 90 percent fatal on the battlefield and now in this case, he gave Quincy even fewer odds.

After cleaning away more of the foul debris, Silas's past experience prohibited his closing the exterior wound of Quincy's abdomen. After brief deliberation, he chose to just close the small but gaping wound in the bowel with thread hoping to keep additional bowel contents from leaking out. With that completed, he simply applied warm clean oil-soaked dressings over the open but now much cleaner abdominal wound. With bowed head, Silas offered a silent prayer for the young man lying before him that was in critical condition. Quincy, while remaining in shock but now sedated from the opiate, was made as comfortable as possible on a narrow litter of buffalo hide located in a small office room.

My uncle and I held out little hope for Quincy's survival. We knew that fever and severe infection were inevitable, and death was likely within hours. I can well remember our sharing continuous observation at the boy's bedside night and day. We made every effort to keep the young man pain-free with frequent large doses of opiates. We knew we were fighting impossible odds.

As expected, Quincy's condition continued to deteriorate rapidly over the following two and a half days. Our constant vigil was maintained as we had planned. The anticipated ragging fever and infection ensued within a few short hours. With our continued use of opiates, Quincy was permitted to remain asleep most of the time. When he did awake, we urged he take sips of cool water.

Some time after the second night's twelfth hour, Quincy died in his customary and induced feverish sleep. Silas contacted Thaddeus Moore, requesting the boy be given the dignity of a simple burial in the local cemetery. The self-proclaimed undertaker moved the young man's lifeless, blanket-covered body from our medical office early that morning.

It was common knowledge throughout town of the drover's catastrophic injury and the continuous care we were providing him in our office. For some prominent Sedalia merchants however; color of the young drover's skin remained of significant importance. After a catastrophic war over the issue, we found that there still remained in Sedalia some long-standing and deep feelings that the war never erased from the minds of several. Quincy's tragic injury and death began to raise turmoil again. Several of Sedalia's influential merchants, known to have been strong Union supporters, were quick to make their views public following news of the boy's death. Under no circumstances were they going to permit Thaddeus to conduct the black man's burial in the local city cemetery alongside their white folk friends and neighbors.

Silas was overwhelmed with anger when receiving word of their rejection for the young man's planned burial. I had never witnessed him to become so upset. There was never a spark of unkindness, selfishness, or ill will shown by Doctor Silas Watson's character since his arrival in Sedalia. Nevertheless, the kind doctor was a man of strong conviction for what he believed proper. The town folks knew him to be intelligent, trustworthy and of sound judgment. Yet, there was no backing down by the small but obviously influential town group.

Without offering any public response on the matter, but with forbearance, Silas instructed Thaddeus to transport Quincy's ravaged body out side of town to the O'Breck farm for its burial. The

O'Breck family had been our patients and friends since we had first arrived in Sedalia. Following our request, Mr. O'Breck had graciously permitted us to arrange for a simple grave on his homestead property. The entire family found this acceptable. My uncle and I were most grateful for Mr. O'Breck's understanding. As doctors, we had been unable to save the young man's life, but we were determined to provide him with a simple and decent burial with a small plane grave marker. We were in complete resolve on the matter.

Knowing that some judgmental folks' state of mind never change even after further consideration, Mr. O'Breck offered to prepare the gravesite on a small hill overlooking the creek passing through his farm. Mr. Moore immediately began construction of a simple pine coffin for the deceased Quincy Wade.

Later in the day following his death, only Uncle Silas, Thaddeus Moore, Mr. O'Breck and I were in attendance for Quincy's burial. Silas Watson's compassion and defiant response to the outcry of some city residents would not be soon forgotten in the days and weeks that would follow.

ooooo

A cold late evening rain was turning the city's streets into a soggy quagmire. At Ruthie's House and behind the bedroom #3 door, a very attractive young woman was comforted by listening to the rain falling upon the building's roof. It was the close of the third day following her arrival in Sedalia and subsequent move into Mrs. Moore's comfortable new quarters. She had found the madam warm and pleasant, but certainly all business. With the stormy night, the young new resident hoped it might permit her having a quiet evening alone to relax and rest.

Having just opened her book to read, she was startled by the sudden rap on her door. Now disconcerted, she scarcely opened it for a glance into the dimly lighted hallway. She recognized Ruthie standing outside her door with a gentleman at the madam's side. The dimmed light in the hall did not permit a good view of the man.

"My dear, this young gentleman has requested that he might see you this evening. He has plans for fewer than thirty minutes, so I'm sure you'll be happy to give him pleasure. I'll talk with you later."

After Ruthie cast a wink at her new lady occupant, she permitted the man's entrance into the bedroom. Without further comment, she left quickly, closing the door behind her.

The bedroom's oil lamp now cast better light on a lean man of medium height. He appeared quite young and remained silent while standing before his chosen lady of pleasure. For a long moment he stood before her staring and taking in her beauty. But then without cause, his face took on a vitriolic expression that could be recognized in his drunken glassy eyes. Maintaining his continued silence and strange demeanor, he seemed to begin viewing the woman with growing indignation. The very attractive woman could only contemplate the man's next move or comment while standing silently before him in her shear colorful nightdress.

Suddenly, he tossed his crumpled wet hat aside onto a nearby chair and began to disrobe hastily. When naked, he stood poised before her and for the first time spoke with husky and slurred speech, obviously tempered by drink.

"Well, pretty lady, I'm here for you to entertain. Ruthie says you're the best in town, so let's get it started." By now, the woman was already becoming repulsed by a combination odor of horses and whiskey that had accompanied the drunken young man and by now was permeating her room.

Without forewarning or additional comment, he suddenly lunged forward at the startled prostitute grabbing and tearing her gown off one shoulder and exposing her breast. With another violent move, he pushed her slender body across the bed and began to force her legs apart. Now fearful and with desperation, she fought to oppose his further advances. With growing anger, she clenched her fist tightly and issued forth several desperate blows across the drunken man's face. Despite her continued efforts to free herself from his grasp, her resistance was no match for his overpowering strength. A vicious attack followed.

"Lay down, you dirty bitch!" he hollered and with repeated blows slashed at the woman's head and face with his open hand.

Now horrified and crying out with pain, she tried again to free herself from his attack. As suddenly as his violent and senseless assault had begun, it ended. For whatever reason, he abruptly quitted his abuse but continued his cursing obscenities. The drover released his vice-like grip on her and clumsily raised himself up from the bed. When he had gained his feet and was upright, he retrieved his filthy clothing and began to dress.

"You're a damn lousy whore, lady!" he yelled. "I paid that madam out there a week's wages to have you! Goddamn you, bitch." While continuing with vile cursing and mumbling, he finished pulling on his clothes and boots after which he swaggered out the bedroom door slamming it loudly behind. In the hallway, his yelling continued, "Goddamn bitch, you can go to hell for all I care!"

Overhearing the boisterous cursing and commotion, Madam Ruthie rushed to investigate. She saw the cowboy leaving by the rear parlor door and stairway leading down to the dark rainy Coffin Alley, still cursing loudly.

Ruthie threw open the door to bedroom 3 and was mortified when seeing her lady renter's bloodied and swollen face still showing lingering fear. She continued weeping all the while clutching a pillow to her chest.

"What in hell's name did that bastard do to you, my dear?" Ruthie angrily cried out as she rushed to console the young woman. Her beaten and now bloodied face was beginning to show evidence of increasing swelling and bruising. A small amount of blood could be seen coming from her nose and from several scratches across her face. Lay down, my dear child, and I'll fetch Doc to come see you right away."

ooooo

I was aware of flattering comments occasionally spread and heard around town about Ruthie's House, but I never knew which had truth or were merely local babble. Little doubt remained from talk on the street that Thaddeus and Ruthie Moore were prospering quite well from their combined business ventures. By all indications and hearsay, Ruthie's House was the classiest bordello in Sedalia, and none of the several others could compare.

The rain was falling quite heavily when Thaddeus escorted me down Coffin Alley and directed me to the narrow stairway leading up to his wife's profitable and well-patronized brothel. I climbed the rain-soaked wooden stairs, somewhat concerned for what I might find. I waited at the top of the stairs a few moments before Mrs. Moore answered my knock and bid me enter the elegant and strikingly appointed small parlor with extra high ceiling and elegant chandelier. I must admit I quickly found the small room's general effect to be most comfortable and pleasing to say the least.

"Good evening, Doctor. Thank you so much for coming. One of my ladies has just been attacked and injured by a drunken fool. Please follow me." The madam, quite elegant in her own right, led me through the parlor and into a short narrow hallway. We stopped outside door #3.

Before opening it, Mrs. Moore implored in a hushed voice, "Please check her over real good, Doc. She is new in town and has only been with me a few days. I'm quite sure you are aware that I demand only the most respectable clientele, so tonight I am most distressed and totally embarrassed that this unfortunate incident could possibly have taken place at all. I do beg your indulgence for my having to call you to my highly respectable place of business under these terms and also for disturbing you on such a rainy night."

She opened the door, and I followed her into the room. "The doctor is here to see you, darling. I'll leave you in his professional hands. Is there anything you might want before I leave you and the kind doctor?"

My patient was reclining on her side with her back to me and sobbing quietly. I removed my wet coat and placed it and my grip on a chair next to the bed.

Mrs. Moore handed me a clean and pressed cotton towel and then made her quick exit leaving me standing at the woman's bedside. Hearing the room door close, my patient slowly turned over to face me.

For unbelievably long silent moments, she and I could only look at one another in sobering disbelief. We were completely stunned and overwhelmed. I tried to speak, but there were no words. I could feel my body beginning to tremble. Finally, I found the courage to speak, "Liz, Oh my god!"

"Oh, my dear Somers. Am I dreaming? Is it really you? I can't believe it's you!" The unexpected shock and confusion was over whelming for her and tears welled in her already puffy and bruised eyes when she recognized who was standing beside her bed.

I grasped her soft hand and felt the nervous tension and excitement rushing through her body and mine. "Liz, you've been hurt. I must examine your face and head. Are you hurting any other place? I must be assured you have no serious injuries," I admonished while trying hard not to convey my profound anxiety and confusion.

I began by gently wiping away the blood that had dried on her forehead and cheek as well as the tears continuing to cascade down her swollen face using the cotton towel the madam had given me. Beneath the dried blood and bruises, her natural beauty remained just as I remembered it on that day so long before when we parted in Saint Louis.

Despite my bewildered state of mind, I fought desperately to maintain a professional manner while continuing my deliberate examination of her face to dispel the presence of any fractures. Believing there were none, I studied each of her facial wounds and found them to be scratches with none likely to cause scar. Discoloration and swelling had already begun to set in, especially beneath one of her eyes. I was finally comfortable that she had weathered the obviously brutal assault without serious injury.

"Somers, I can't tell you what this means to see you again. I believed you to be in Columbia."

Once again mustering my most professional tone of voice I admonished, "Liz, I find nothing seriously wrong, but I do want you to drink this medicine after I leave. It will provide you some relief of your discomfort and provide you some sleep. The medicine is in this small bottle that I'm placing on this chest by your bed. On some other time perhaps we can meet again and share what has happened in each of our lives since those memorable days we shared while on the train. At that moment, I could simply find nothing more to say. My confused mind and nervous state would only allow me to awkwardly retrieve my grip and coat. I knew I must leave quickly.

"Good night, Somers. No, no—that's wrong! I must call you Dr. Watson. It's so wonderful to see you. We must meet soon. I know we have so much to share after all this time."

As I descended the stairway into the dark wet alley, my mind was filled not only with disgust, but most of all, complete mystery and confusion. What I had just witnessed brought a pall over me and my heart was racing. The cold rainy drizzle continued as I found my way through the infamous alley then onto the board-covered walkway. Ohio Street had become a sea of mud with the prolonged rain and had only a few pedestrians except for me.

As I walked along, my thoughts were solely consumed with the patient I'd just left. My body remained tense and my mind was already beginning to fill with questions for which I wanted and needed answers. I was in agreement with Liz. We must meet again, but in privacy and certainly some place other than Ruthie's House. After reaching home, I had become totally oblivious to the cold wet night.

As I fell into bed I remained filled with nervous exhaustion, but was sure that sleep wasn't going to come easily. I was determined to learn so much more about the woman for whom I had kept such fond memories for so long. Liz Cromwell had a great deal to explain. I hoped it could be soon.

17

A few years prior to the war, James O'Breck and his large family moved to Missouri from Massachusetts. For several months before their leaving Massachusetts, they shared a dream of homesteading property on the frontier, possibly in Missouri. They were industrious, religious, and peace loving Irish descendants. When leaving Massachusetts, there were six children. Tragedy befell them in a somewhat desolate area of countryside in eastern Ohio. Four-year-old Jessica Mae accidentally fell from their wagon and her small body was crushed beneath one of the wagon's heavy wheels.

Overcome with grief, James and his eldest son buried little Jessica in a tiny grave in a field nearby. With overwhelming grief and heavy hearts after the tragic loss of their little Jessica, the remaining family members pressed on toward the Missouri frontier.

They found an area to homestead near a small community of immigrant settlers, some of whom were also Irish. They were thrilled having found the place of their dreams. It was 160 acres of rich bottom land, a portion of which bordered a narrow creek, a branch of the Flat River. The property was located less than four miles north and west of the settlement that would later become known as Sedalia.

After spending days selecting and then cutting timber from off their newly acquired property, the family set about the task of building a spacious log house. When it was finally completed, they began construction of a large barn to shelter their oxen team, a milk cow, and three horses. The barn had space for hay storage during the winter months. They added a small shed sometime later for their flock of chickens. An often-used trail passed by their property leading southeast to the growing settlement of immigrants, soon to become a town.

The family worked the soil and planted corn on most of the open acres. With persistent local talk of approaching war in the area, the family chose to keep their personal views regarding the slavery issue to themselves; however, privately it was their wish to remain neutral. The family carried on with the traditional rural lifestyle typical for the times, but always with Jessica in their memory wishing that she could be with them to enjoy their new home in Missouri.

Over the years that followed, James and his happy family made many new friends in the area and became quite successful crop farmers. James spent a brief period as a volunteer in the Missouri Union militia early in the war. Like so many in the Sedalia area, the family always remained fearful of a guerilla attack. The senseless ambush warfare that was occurring in several areas in the state during the Civil War brought unrest for many residents who continued in their attempts to simply remain neutral regarding the slave problem.

Before their move west, a major bank in Boston had provided James with financial credit for expenses incurred on the family's planned trip west and in finally securing a homestead. Unfortunate circumstances followed soon after the close of the Civil War. James's family as with most of their neighbors and friends suffered significant financial hardship with the unforeseen plummet in commodity prices. To make the problem even worse, at the very same time there was a corresponding sudden rise in bank interest rates. The local economy was collapsing and was creating panic and turmoil for everyone.

After a prolonged period of financial struggle, the O'Breck's had no other choice in the matter and were forced to have their beloved farm booked for public auction on the steps of Sedalia's courthouse. On the appointed auction day James and his wife stood on the courthouse steps with several of their neighbors watching their farms being sold. Tears filled the eyes of many as they watched the sad proceedings taking place.

On that same late summer day Uncle Silas and I were having a relaxing stroll down Ohio Street. From some distance away we took witness of the growing crowd gathered outside the courthouse. Curiosity befell us both. Perhaps some accident might have occurred. We could not recall hearing about any special event. After a brief pause watching from across the street, we became more inquisitive and finally crossed over and joined in.

We were reminded quickly by onlookers the reason for the gathering. Hearing earlier about the auction, it had slipped from our minds. Ironically, for several months, Uncle Silas and I had shared our thoughts and discussed possible purchase of farm property in the area having hope it might supplement our practice income. Now, after watching and hearing the properties being auctioned, serious thought of possible farm ownership was quickly rekindled.

On good authority, we had learned some time before the O'Breck farm was suffering from financial problems like many farms at the time and that it might become available for sale sometime in the future. We were well acquainted with the farm's convenient location since we had on occasion made several home visits when the children had become ill. In this way, we had become close friends with the hard-working family and had become aware of how close-knit they were. Through their effort over the years, they had developed and maintained a very nice and handsome piece of property. Through our shared friendship, the family had also provided a final resting place for Quincy Wade that had meant a great deal to my uncle and me.

Later that morning, the James O'Breck property was announced for auction. To my surprise, Silas turned to me with a smile and said, "Let's do it!"

Moments later, to our mutual joy, our final bid was accepted! It was at first somewhat hard to comprehend, but we had suddenly become the new owners of the O'Breck property. It wasn't until the following day when we learned more about the family's problems and their severe financial plight. With our already solicitous feelings for the O'Breck family and the fact we now owned the farm they had developed and loved, Silas and I agreed to make them an offer.

Our offer was to allow the family to continue living and operating the farm as if it were their own. In the future, they would be obliged to pay us whatever they were capable from the farm's yearly income. My uncle and I remained confident that commodity prices would rise again in the future and when they did, the family would be capable for making the farm profitable.

The entire family was overwhelmed with joy and happiness when hearing our offer. It would permit them to remain living on the property on which they had worked so hard and had come to love. With profound gratitude, they accepted our offer. Uncle Silas and I felt good knowing that we were not just the family's doctors but also landowners with remarkable tenants. It was going to be an exciting new experience for my medical partner and for me.

ooooo

On a cloudy humid Sunday morning not long after we had purchased the farm and the legalities were completed, the O'Breck family had already left to attend church services in town—that is, all except sixteen-year-old Joshua. He was not feeling well that morning so had remained at home. The well-favored young boy felt assured that with his feeling ill and then receiving his father's permission to remain home from church, it would not only provide him some extra sleep but a possible reprieve from performing his customary livestock chores later in the day.

With the family gone and after returning to bed, Josh was startled by a thundering knock on the front cabin door. The sleepy but startled boy knew it to be most unlikely for his family to have Sunday morning guests since each Sunday morning was always reserved only for attending church services in town. Now awake and with due concern, he grabbed the armed .44-caliber pistol kept by his bed and cautiously approached the door.

Before opening the door, he called out, "Who is it?"

"Don't give a mind 'bout that. Is your father in there?" a deep voice questioned from outside the door.

"No, sir, the family's at church. Why do you want my father?"

Josh was now filled with guarded curiosity. Keeping his gun concealed, he cautiously opened the door just wide enough to permit his seeing the gentleman on the outside with the deep voice.

Some distance away, Josh saw two other men on horseback silently waiting beneath a huge oak tree in the yard. Each was armed with gun rigs on their waist and rifles housed in their respective saddle scabbards.

With growing concern, Josh's attention returned and made special witness of the large stocky man standing at the doorway. The most immediate and notable feature was a black cloth patch covering his right eye. The wide brim of his soiled hat was resting low just above his brow. A large figured blue and white stampede rag hung draped around his broad neck. He had a large heavy and unkempt gray beard covering most of his otherwise tanned face. His blouse and trousers appeared covered with dirt and dried mud. He wore large heavy spurs attached to his boots also showing evidence of dried mud. Josh noted a pearl-handled large caliber pistol resting in the well-worn leather gun rig attached around his waist.

"My father will be back sometime after church, mister. You'll have to come back later to talk with him."

Both men on horseback continued their vigilance in complete silence. Without further comment, the stranger turned and retreated to his waiting horse. Having quickly closed the door, Josh was totally unaware of which direction the men chose when leaving. He naturally assumed they had left by the front road. However, in reality they had descended the small hill next to the cabin and had stopped by the barn.

Pondering the men's business in wanting his father, the boy had returned to bed after placing his pistol within easy reach beneath his feathered pillow. Suddenly, Josh became aware of several unusually loud snorts and whinnies coming from horses down by the barn. He could tell by their sound they were the family's horses and that they obviously had been disturbed by something. He jumped from his bed and rushed to a cabin window to investigate.

Josh saw the three unwelcomed visitors down by the barn. The large man's two silent comrades could be seen leading the O'Breck's three horses from inside the barn. Josh saw that both ox and old milk cow had already been turned loose. The man with the eye patch had dismounted and was in the act of setting afire loose hay lying just inside the barn entrance. While Josh continued watching in horror and anger, he saw the entire barn rapidly becoming engulfed in smoke and flames.

By now Josh was seething in hatred watching the deliberate theft and destruction occurring before his eyes. At that moment, he recalled his father's teachings about the precepts of duty. He grabbed his pistol and rushed outside the cabin. The outlaws had already made their escape down the road in full gallop with the family's three stolen horses reining at side. The boy lost sight of them as they disappeared down the front hill and by now well beyond his gun range.

Now, Josh felt powerless and sick of heart. As he turned to view the burning barn, huge flames were licking at its overhead timbers and he could hear the crackling sounds of burning wood. Tears of hate and vengeance welled in the boy's eyes.

For nearly a week after that fateful Sunday morning, the barn's timbers and hay continued to smolder with intermittent small plumbs of smoke rising from the carnage. Each night when darkness descended upon the scene, an eerie red glow could be seen coming from the persistent slow-burning timbers and small hot coals Later that week, a welcomed rain shower finally extinguished the last of the burning embers. An ugly burned skeleton with heaped piles of ash and debris was all that remained.

When hearing the awful news of the theft and destruction out at the farm, Silas and I were incensed with confusion and anger. Josh gave the city marshal and folks in the area a description of the three highwaymen and their mounts.

Vigilante crimes of a like nature had not been unusual in the Sedalia area at the time. At many sites within the state, similar crimes were occurring with frequency and proved nearly impossible to prevent. No one had a discernible explanation why our property had been targeted. The peace loving and God fearing O'Breck family had never offered sympathetic feelings either for or against slavery to anyone. The same was true for Uncle Silas and for me.

ooooo

A few weeks later, Uncle Silas was enjoying a relaxing stroll along the creek one day while visiting the farm. Suddenly, the lonely haunting sound of a barn owl caught his attention. It had come from a tall tree on a grassy ridge overlooking the creek below. When directing his sight toward the tree from where the sound had come, something much more important caught his immediate attention. It was the small wooden cross marking Quincy Wade's gravesite that he had asked Thaddeus to make the day after the boy's burial. Little doubt now remained in the doctor's mind. The mystery that had plagued him for weeks was solved!

The hateful and senseless crime committed that Sunday morning had resulted from just one individual's actions, and that was his very own. *He* was the one person that had displayed infinite anger and displeasure with the city's merchants rejecting Quincy's burial in the city cemetery. Once word had spread around town that Doc Watson had responded by having the black man buried on the farm property could only mean he was a sympathizer and "nigger lover"!

Each piece of the puzzle was falling into place. Moments later when Silas was standing next to Quincy's grave, he looked down at the small unmarked cross. It told him why he had remained undaunted in his conviction that Quincy Wade deserved his peaceful resting place regardless of his skin color. The aging doctor remained at peace knowing that at any another time, he would have done absolutely nothing different.

18

Liz Cromwell was filled with emotion and uncertainty when entering the doctor's office waiting area for her meeting with Somers that morning. Her mere presence in his office had created for her considerable anxiety and fear. Yet, she was more than anxious to see and to talk to Somers again. She had purposefully worn a borrowed over-sized bonnet, trusting that it might help in keeping her identity hidden from public view. As she sat waiting to visit with Somers, her heart was racing.

When I entered my office that morning, I saw Liz seated across the small room. Her anxiety was easy to discern. Hoping to allay her fears, I bid her a cordial good morning. It was easy to appreciate her anxiety as I watched her take a seat across from my desk. I must admit that I also harbored similar feelings at that moment.

Conscious of her emotional state, I opened the conversation in what I hoped would bring some comfort to her since I had no intentions for our meeting to become moralistic in nature. My mind had remained confused and deeply saddened since our meeting that night in Ruthie's House, yet I could never renounce my personal feelings for the woman. My questions simply needed answers.

"Liz, I'm grateful for your coming. Since that night in your room, I have been anxious for us to become reacquainted and share our personal thoughts and experiences since saying our good-byes in Saint Louis. Needless to say, I was taken aback when I discovered that you were here in Sedalia. I had assumed you were living and working with the banker's children. Please share with me what has happened to you since our parting at the train depot."

While I detected in her some hesitation, she responded slowly with a soft but saddened voice, "I had told you of my opportunity and plans for becoming the wealthy family's governess. Following my successful interview, I began my work with the children. The parents provided me with comfortable quarters in the spacious and very elegant home. I found their three children delightful. I was treated with kindness and respect for nearly three years, but then everything began to turn bad for me which I never expected could happen. That was when the father began causing me to be very uneasy whenever he was near. I've never known his reason, but it began with his impolite and bawdy comments; then his vulgarity increased with time."

"What did he do or say that upset you so?"

"At first, whenever he was near and we happened to be alone someplace in the house, he would begin placing his hands on me in an inappropriate and unseemly manner all the while continuing his foul and discourteous comments. Oh, Somers! No person had ever done or said such things to me like that. At first, I tried taking little notice of his actions, but as time passed, he became more forceful and demanding. I didn't know what to do or say since I wished to continue my work with the children.

One evening when his missus was not at home and the children were in bed, he entered my quarters without forewarning and chanced to see me disrobed. Being much stronger than I, he forced me onto my bed against my will and then violated me. After having his pleasure, he said he'd kill me if I ever made mention to his missus or anyone about what took place."

Hearing her story was causing me anger, but I continued giving solace to my friend. "What did you do next?"

"It was two days later when the missus confronted me. She was distraught and filled with anger and hate. Never before had she acted towards me in that manner. She said her husband had told her that I was a wicked temptress and had been trying to seduce him whenever I might have the occasion. He told her I was an evil bitch and that I must depart from his house immediately.

Their manservant moved my belongings out of the house the following morning. I was left with a small amount of money with no place to go."

"Liz, for God's sake, how and why did you come here to Sedalia?"

"Somers, I was without a husband, without work, and with very little money. I had few choices. I could not find work. My body was the only thing I knew that could support me, and it has. Regardless of the displeasure and heartache my situation brings, my body responds to what I ask of it, and it has become my salvation.

Two or three days after wandering on the streets and now without money for food, a gentleman asked for my favor. I was left with no choice. That was the start of my business. While in Saint Louis, I'd heard of this town's reputation for women of my kind. After saving some money, I came here on the train. A saloon owner told me to see Mrs. Moore. Ruthie took me in and has been most kind and understanding."

Having listened intently to her disquieting story, I could only remain silent just trying to comprehend the heartache and circumstances that had befallen my friend. Now with my stirring emotions, I found it impossible to find the right words to respond, so I had no choice but to begin directing the conversation to myself.

"After my leaving you and Waldo in Saint Louis, I moved on to Columbia as planned to join my uncle's practice. After my arrival, he informed me of his wife's tragic death a few days after his return home from the war. At that time, I found Uncle Silas filled with bitterness and despair. However, after time and our joining together in practice, I observed him to begin developing renewed enthusiasm.

It was several weeks later when I learned that his unrelenting despair and grief had prompted thoughts of leaving Columbia with all of its recent sadness and memories. He hoped to move elsewhere and begin again. He offered his practice to me, but I was more interested in remaining with him in his new adventure. We chose Sedalia, and our practice has done well. Now fate has brought you and me together once again under the most surprising and troubling circumstance."

Following the conclusion of my own story and without uttering a word, Liz suddenly rose up and drew herself close to me. She cupped my face in her hands and rendered me an impassioned kiss. I could see that her eyes were beginning to fill with tears. Quickly, she turned and without comment, quietly left my office.

Her fervent and surprising response following our brief conversation left me dumbfounded. I had no misgiving, and truth be told, I had continued having sensuous feelings for Liz Cromwell since the moment of our first meeting. Now my feelings had become a profound mixture of lament, anger, and disappointment.

Hereafter and with deep regret, I would only come to view my friend as a ruined woman. My fondest memories of Liz Cromwell would be difficult for me to forget. I knew the beautiful sweet woman for whom I had so much affection would live in my memory for a very long time.

ooooo

Almost three months had passed since the Sunday morning guerrilla raid on the farm. By then, with help from neighbors, the industrious O'Breck family had nearly completed construction on the new barn. With no sighting or other word about the three marauding Jayhawkers, we assumed they had moved on, possibly joining with another group.

Having already turned sixteen, young Josh O'Breck had other thoughts. He was unable to erase the picture in his mind of the three men stealing the horses and the barn engulfed in flames that morning. Josh was rapt on gaining retaliation in some way. With pistol in hand and against his parents' will, he left home to join with a local group who was committed to protecting other settlers' property from looting and destruction.

Raids had become commonplace, and Josh was hopeful that he and his group might find the man with the eye patch and his two loathing comrades. In Josh's mind, he had a deadly score to settle.

ooooo

Three of the youngest Johnson kids had broken out with a rash and fever. Mrs. Johnson suspected their illness to be the measles, but she told her husband she would have peace of mind if Doctor Watson looked in on them.

Shortly after noon on a bright but somewhat cool day, Silas left the office in his buggy on the five-mile trip to the Johnson farm east of town. He was enjoying the refreshing cool breeze rushing past his face as the buggy carried him smoothly along the narrow country road. As was his custom, he was humming a favorite tune with his thoughts far away.

Suddenly, his attention was drawn just ahead to the presence of two men on horseback and partially concealed by shrubs and brush alongside the road. Silas believed they were attempting to hide in a deep cutback only a short distance off the road. As he drew nearer, the two men made their sudden presence up onto the road forcing Silas's buggy to an abrupt halt. Both men had pistols drawn and had them directed at the bewildered doctor.

One shouted out, "We know who ya are, Doc. You're that nigger lover!"

Their unexpected intrusion and the man's verbal accusation brought Silas intense anger as he began studying his assailants more closely. When the shaken doctor noted the black eye patch on the larger of the two men, it brought to mind Josh O'Breck's description weeks before. This was the same loathed character that had set fire to the barn and then stole the horses. This man fit Josh's description perfectly, but Silas could not recall the boy's description of the other two comrades present that Sunday morning. At the moment, he could not identify the accompanying rider.

With gained courage, Silas retorted, "I don't take kindly to your calling me that. What do ya want? I'm on my way to see some sick kids. Now let me pass." Silas tried not to imply his growing fear, realizing he was without protection since he had mistakenly left his pistol at home.

"Well, Doc, we know not only who you are but what you are. You got that nigger boy buried out there on your farm and then, ya even marked his damn grave. We know 'cause we were out there one day and saw it for ourselves. Now, you get yourself down off that there fancy buggy."

After issuing his command, the assailant wearing the eye patch quickly dismounted and began to release the reata that was attached to his saddle. At that moment, Silas heard the loud *click* as the other man drew back the hammer on his pistol. Brazenly, he began waving the weapon around in the air and then drew aim at Silas while commanding in a loud voice, "Hey, Doctor, I said get your skinny ass down off your nice black buggy... *now!*"

Silas recognized unquestioned seriousness in both men, and suspected both of having hair-trigger temperaments and quite prepared to shoot at any provocation. Having no choice, Silas slowly rose up from his buggy seat and cautiously stepped down onto the road. With body trembling, he used the front buggy wheel to gain support while waiting for what the two desperados had in mind. Silas was beginning to believe any negotiations seemed highly unlikely.

The grizzled one-eyed assailant quickly dropped the loop of his reata over Silas's head and drew it tight against his body with both arms secured behind his back. With the remaining length of rope, he bound the trembling doctor's body tightly against the buggy wheel.

Now unnerved and quite aware of the doctor's peril, his faithful mare gave a sudden snort followed with a loud whinny. She began pawing the dirt with her front hooves and repeated her whinny. She left little doubt of her perception of the situation at hand.

"Well, Doc, I guess by now you understand we've got no goddamn use for sympathizers who love those nigger folks. Have ya got anythin' to say, Watson?" the man on horseback growled.

Now realizing full well the dials of his busy and once happy life were showing their hands to be resting very near the midnight hour, Silas was suddenly overcome with a serene and willful peace that was beginning to spread throughout his body. The courageous old gentleman intently studied each of his captors for a long moment before issuing his response.

"During the war as a doctor, I gave four years of my life to the needs of the sick and horribly injured Union soldiers—and yes, on occasion, to men and boys fighting for the South's cause as well. The men and boys from both sides were fighting and dying in a damn bloody war over issues for which they each held strong but quite opposite regard. Thanks to the Lord Almighty, the war is finally over and the slave issue has come to an honorable settlement as judged by most folks, yet each of you appear to have no concern for what our country went through. Yes, I treated that badly injured boy whose skin was a different color than yours and mine. When the Lord finally saw fit to take him, he deserved the right for a proper burial and I saw fit that he got one. I have no shame for my actions either then or now. I hope your sons and daughters never face the hate that boy endured from men like yourselves. That's all I've got to say except… maybe the Lord will still try and save your miserable souls."

The serene countryside was suddenly shaken with the thundering sound of two consecutive shots from a large caliber pistol. Moments later, two vengeful men spurred their horses and fled full-gallop from the despicable scene. Neither man was ever seen nor heard from again in Pettis County, Missouri.

Sadness and bitter outrage erupted when the shocking news of the doctor's murder spread throughout Sedalia and the county. I was incensed with heartache, confusion, and anger when given the news of my uncle's fate. A neighbor of the Johnsons had come upon the shocking scene and found the doctor's lifeless body lashed to his buggy at the side of the road. From all appearances, the bridled mare had begun to drag the buggy with her dead master some distance along the dirt road.

Engulfed with my personal grief, I turned to Thaddeus Moore for his assistance in making the proper arrangements for Silas's burial at the farm. I requested that he plan to have my uncle's grave placed next to Quincy's since there was little doubt in my mind as to where Silas would want to have his eternal rest.

Thaddeus immediately began construction on an exceptionally beautiful coffin and took charge of the funeral details for me. My sadness kept me from taking care of necessary business I knew was at hand. Several of Sedalia's prominent businessmen began questioning why the town's honorable doctor was not going to be buried in the city cemetery. Hearing their comments made it very difficult for me not to give an ungracious response, but I remained hopeful that after each of them had given their mindless questions more thought, the logical and truthful answer would come forth.

ooooo

Much like what occurred to Silas in Columbia following his wife's suicide, I began to experience similar misgivings about my remaining in Sedalia. With the calamity of Liz Cromwell's revelation closely followed by my dear uncle's senseless and shocking murder, I found it difficult to sort things out in my mind and to concentrate on the medical practice for which I was now responsible. Those problems brought despair and I began to lose interest in our town and Pettis County.

Anger and bitter disappointment resulting from events over which I had no control created much confusion for me. I began to question where my own life was heading. Leaving the sad gripping memories I had experienced in Sedalia and moving farther west, perhaps to Texas, seemed like a possible solution. It was a solution worthy of my studied consideration.

With my sole inheritance of both properties following Uncle Silas's death, a move from Sedalia meant far-reaching legal questions to resolve. Neither property would provide me with lasting interest after my leaving town. Knowing of my uncle's love for the farm and his admiration and respect for the family, it seemed only appropriate that they should receive return ownership. Placing the property for public sale would serve the family no useful purpose. With my uncle's grave on the property, he would always remain with the folks he had admired and loved.

After an especially busy and tiring day, after going to bed that night I found difficulty in getting to sleep. At some time before sunrise and after finally falling asleep, I experienced having a mysterious dream. Now fully awake later that morning, I was still able to recall vivid details of the dream. Strangely, it brought me a great deal to ponder in the days that followed. Although the dream seemed plausible, it remained filled with a discordant solution to my problem. Nevertheless, I found it worthy of my continued careful consideration.

ooooo

Following my Uncle Silas's death, I continued with my practice in Sedalia for five years—much longer than I had anticipated. The murderous culprits were never found. During those five years, the baffling dream never left me. In truth, I was unable to bring it to the fore as a proper and satisfactory conclusion to my problem.

During that time, I continued watching Sedalia grow with the construction of several one- and two-story businesses in the center of town along with a number of private dwellings. Despite its growth and cultural improvements, Sedalia remained a rough town with its inherent problems with vice. Also during those five years, the city was plagued with several serious fires that destroyed some businesses. The courthouse and the popular opera house were two of those important city landmarks destroyed by fire; however, the community responded quickly with new construction.

The MK&T Railroad Company continued its growth as did railroad expansion elsewhere in the country. Katy's connection with Saint Louis brought additional new growth for our town. Prostitution and other vices were an unrelenting problem due to the continued flow of transients through town. However, after the opening of several other cattle trails, especially the Chisholm, the size and number of drives arriving in Sedalia diminished significantly.

Once having made my decision to leave Sedalia and move on to Texas, I spent nearly six months in preparation. I dealt with the legal matters relating to the farm and city properties. With the O'Breck family having become financially prosperous once again, I transferred complete ownership back to them. They were over joyed and most appreciative to regain ownership of the farm they had always loved.

I had rarely seen or talked with Liz other than our perchance meetings on the street. I was aware that she was still working at Ruthie's House. Meanwhile, I was finding the city property a more difficult problem to resolve. After much thought and loss of sleep, I finally reached a decision as to how I might deal with the problem.

I sent a message to Ruthie Moore requesting that she send Liz to my office since I had a private matter I wished to discuss with her. Later that day, Liz appeared as I had requested. When entering my office, I could see that she was filled with anxiety much like what I had witnessed before. This time, she had all the earmarks of being even more troubled and anxious.

"Please sit down and allay your troubled mind, Liz. After having given it much thought, I have something to bandy about with you."

After her first visit in my office years before and sharing her innermost intimate revelation, I was sure she had misgiving that we would ever speak again. Now, there was a state of confusion written across her pretty face.

I began our conversation by apprising her of my eminent plans for leaving Sedalia. "I am leaving for several reasons, which I do not choose to discuss at this time. As you might have guessed, I became the sole heir to this property and the farm following my uncle's death. Having made plans to leave Sedalia and my medical practice, a problem arises which I hope you will be interested in helping me solve.

Several years ago I listened with concern when you told me how your plight in Saint Louis had given rise to such a change in your life. Liz, since our first meeting, I have kept strong sentiments for you. Now, it would be of comfort to me for you to give consideration to my proposal. It's a plan I could never have offered to you before the present time."

Tears began to well in her large blue eyes. Despite her tears, I could see she had become more relaxed and was listening intently. I continued, "Should you be interested and willing, I would like to deed this property to you but only with certain constraints. Your solemn promise to comply with my demands is imperative and should benefit you. Should you not wish to make such a covenant and then uphold it, I will retract my offer."

"But Somers, why do you wish to help me? I have done nothing to make you proud or given you reason to love or care for me. What my life has become is of my own making. Long ago, I had no choices and knew no other way."

She now became more emotional and gave way to sobbing. I could feel her chagrin while trying to discuss the matter with me. I began having misgivings whether I should even mention my proposal. I paused for a long moment desperately searching for the right words and to be certain she did not misconstrue my demands of her.

"Being well aware of your situation, I want to make my offer which has required much thought. I am willing to deed my property to you under the proviso that you will make use of the property for it to become an upstanding boarding house business. My demands would be for you to accept full responsibility for its management and daily operation.

What's more, my second proviso is that you must change your manner of life and thus relinquish yourself and your new business from the grave moral failing that is so prevalent in Sedalia. Do you understand? Once your business has become successful, I would expect compensation as you can arrange. Above all, it's my wish this new business would bring a change to your life for the future and that you might find renewed happiness hereafter. Please give this your sincere consideration. Be certain that you would be willing to make the changes in your life that I request. I will await your decision."

19

As early as 1803, the federal government made its initial plans for creating a permanent Indian territory. Thomas Jefferson and others favored such an area where all Native American Indians might remain. In theory it was to be a place where the Indians might govern themselves while being protected from outside land speculators, whiskey purveyors, and unscrupulous traders. They reasoned that the proposed territory should be located well beyond where the growing numbers of white settlers had already begun to homestead. Such homestead land for immigrant settlers was in great demand.

The federal policies that followed for solving the Indian problem created enormous misunderstanding and many new and unexpected problems. There was complete lack of organization for relocating the Indian tribes. The federal government's ignorance and lack of genuine concern for the many differences in culture and customs of the sixty or more Indian tribes was largely responsible for the chaos and bloodshed that would follow in the years to come.

Absence of an organized plan for resettlement became evident when various inducements and bogus treaty negotiations were presented, with most failing miserably. Brutal warfare followed bringing no solution or success to the initial problem. The mindless poor plan for the transition failed to consider each tribe's daily needs. Those needs varied significantly from tribe to tribe. This complete oversight proved critical and a disastrous error.

Federal appointed Indian agents coming from Washington were frequently inept for their job and too many of them lacked any form of righteous or ethical conduct. While many of these agents were simply corrupt and immoral, their human nature and brazen personalities only compounded the problem for which they were assigned to help solve. In the end, the government's only policy and plan for the transition was to move the tribes to their reservations on the Indian Territory. This was to come about by either a volunteer and peaceful basis by each tribe *or* simply move them there with whatever means of force that might become necessary.

Another crucial matter, either totally misunderstood or simply ignored, was the simple fact that virtually all Native Americans were steadfast in their ancient superstitions for which they remained committed to preserve at whatever cost it might be to them. This was especially true concerning their spiritual customs they had always maintained within the respective tribes. The Indians believed strongly in a Great Spirit. It was that honored and beloved Spirit who had created and controlled everything within the world that included the Heavens and the Earth. The Spirit could grant each of them rewards but also could take them away.

In reality, the newly designated Indian Territory was a vast carved out section of land that seemed quite worthless to the government at the time. That land area would eventually become known as the state of Oklahoma. Shortly after the Civil War, the sad and tumultuous relocation of the Native Americans began.

To move the Indians into the designated territory from their scattered locations throughout America proved very costly to the federal treasury as well as being extremely difficult and violent to carry out. Many types of men volunteered for becoming an Indian Fighter, a job that the federal government paid $13.00 a month for enlistees and significantly more for officers. As time would tell, the soldier's work became a mixture of absolute boredom and grave personal danger. However, the men were assured good army food, comfortable lodging plus a clothing allowance. For the reasoning of many volunteers, the advantages the job offered far out weighed any risk of death at the hand of some red man.

During the years that followed, the government funneled vast sums of money into the project. Their reasoning was based on the premise that isolating the tribes would not only ensure safety for travelers, freight and cargo, but would also complete the eventual subjugation of the Indians. However, it was soon discovered that the enormity of the plan had been and was sadly miscalculated in every way.

The "five civilized tribes" gave reference to the Choctaws, Cherokee, Creeks, Chickasaws, and Seminoles. This did seem appropriate since they represented some of the more well-adjusted and peace-abiding tribes. For the most part they chose to remain settled within their respective villages working the surrounding land to grow crops for their sustenance. They were not considered nomadic or hunters.

With the passage of time, members of the five tribes were gradually, although they were found to be stubborn on occasion, moved by military escort from their scattered villages into Indian Territory where they formed their tribal nations. Adaptation had its problems from time to time but eventually proved to be reasonably successful. The Cherokee tribal members labeled their trek to their new location within Indian Territory, a "Trail of Tears".

Dealing with the nomadic and often hostile plains tribes that included the Kiowa, Cheyenne, Arapaho, Apache, and Comanche among others proved with time to be quite another story. These tribes had always been nomadic hunters. They possessed an entirely different mindset, at times even savage. Their transition proved to be dangerously more difficult when compared to the civilized tribes. They were hostile and raged warfare with frequency among themselves and any others. With the persistent encroachment made on them by the white man's fervor for expanding the frontier, he too was to become another enemy with whom they must do battle. These nomadic tribes possessed far different cultures and customs. Basically, they were hunters and peoples that roamed with freedom anytime and anywhere across the plains, always in search for buffalo or wild game for their sustenance.

By their very nature, their warlike character would lead them into brutal inter tribal warfare and create major problems and conflicts with white settlers who were exploiting their territory. Their physical wellbeing and existence depended upon their ability to retain, at all cost, their free rein of the plains country. They were prepared to steal or ambush without provocation from those who might possess what they needed or simply wanted.

The Kiowa and Comanche raided Texas settlements and pillaged caravans of freight and cargo passing over the Santa Fe Trail. The Cheyenne and Sioux made travel on the Oregon and Bozeman Trails especially hazardous.

The plains tribe's Spiritual belief centered upon a great home in the heavens where, after death, their greatest hunting ground would be found. Revenge always brought satisfaction for them. To forgive or show consolation only revealed a weakness on their part. They were unbelievably shrewd, cunning and crafty.

Once having acquired both gun and horse from the white man, each became their most cherished and important possessions. Their horse was coveted by them and considered invaluable. The finer and faster the horseflesh, the greater the pride it generated in the minds of these fearless tribesmen. The Comanche in particular, became exceptional horsemen and extremely adapt when firing their carbine rifle while mounted on the back of their fast of foot pony.

Interestingly, each of the civilized tribes would take from the white man whatever items or mannerisms they found useful or of interest to them. If the item would benefit them in anyway, they found a way to create it. Some items became well known and specifically distinctive for each respective tribe.

Today, it is not difficult to understand why the government experienced so much difficulty forcing the Indian tribes into the confinement of the Indian Territory. One can also understand why it was much easier for the civilized tribes to adapt to the reservation's way of life as compared to the roaming plains tribes. It is also understandable why all Indian tribes continued to find disfavor with their being disrupted by the white man who showed neither compassion nor understanding for their culture. For many, retaliation through savage warfare became the logical response to the demands being placed on them by the white man.

During those troublesome times, it was evident to all tribes what impact the progressive expansion of the Iron Horse's steel tracks were having across "their land", their culture and their future existence. The white man's intense fervor for moving the frontier further and further west became evident to every Native American. The ultimate realization that each Indian and white man possessed their own unique values in life which never could be shared proved to be most important in the end. The Indian and the white man were simply incompatible on every count.

By 1871, any and all treaty negotiations between the government and the tribes had sadly deteriorated to the point where they had become unimportant and passé. The treaties offered little or no value for providing future protection to the troubled Native Americans wherever they might be located. Regrettably, the Treaty at Medicine Lodge that same year hastened the final demise forever for all Native Americans and their customary way of life.

The brazen and callous wording within that treaty made clear to everyone alike of the government's complete disregard for any red man and his culture. With their signatures on that treaty, the white men had boldly declared the final stand taken by the government. Unfortunately, after several years of savage Indian wars and conflicts of retaliation that would follow, the country had reason to regret the treaty's caustic wording.

The growing numbers of European immigrants in America were eager to grasp their share of homestead land that was being offered on the western frontier. In the majority of cases, they registered no sympathy or did they possess any rational understanding of either the Indian or his culture. The government's proviso for the Oklahoma Land Rush of 1889 merely poured fuel to the already existing fire.

Federal Indian Commissioner Hiram Price perhaps best summarized the broiling conflict by proclaiming, "One of two things must eventually take place—either civilization *or* the extermination of the Indians. Savage and civilized life cannot live and prosper on the same ground. One of the two must die." Perhaps nowhere but in Texas would Price's statement become more prophetic in the years that would follow.

ooooo

Indian retribution was certain to come and did! It was merely a matter of time. Documented accounts regarding brutal torture and savagery exist that have their origins from within many of the tribes. Each tribe usually had their own customs in kind and manner for eliciting torture whenever necessary whether against another tribesman or against the hated white man.

The savage taking of a scalp, especially from the white man, was partly for trophy. But it also gave reason for their scalp dance for appeasing the spirits of the dead. Rarely would any man survive after being scalped, but some did and their cases have been documented. Once the victim's scalp was taken, additional torture followed leading to the victim's death.

It has been said some white women preferred being killed by their husbands rather than to be captured by the Indians. Some tribes horribly violated a white woman in any number of ways following her capture. More often, she would become a "white Indian," often the wife of some warrior and remain with the tribe thereafter.

ooooo

In the course of time I had become aware of the many problems Washington was having with the Indians and their resistance in having their culture and domain disrupted. With the crush of settlers moving onto the western frontier and the dynamic changes taking place, I had become somewhat sympathetic for the Indian's problems; however, I also shared sympathy for the white settlers and what savagery they were experiencing in so many locations.

But in truth, my thoughts and concerns remained more with my plans for leaving Sedalia. For several years I had been bent on leaving Sedalia, yet I continued having strong feelings about leaving the medical practice that Silas and I had worked hard to develop. Be that as it may, there was still adventure in my heart, and my decision was finally made for a move to Texas.

There was no misgiving in my mind concerning the farm transfer to the O'Breck family, albeit I had remained solicitous as to the demands I had placed on Liz regarding the city property and her change of life style. I trusted I had not left her at a loss for responding to my demands. I still believed her to be a gracious and righteous woman who had been forced into a circumstance of human frailty from which she was never able to escape. I continued to hold out the possibility that my offer might bring a welcomed change in her life. Regardless of her storied past, I was certain I would always have sentiments and forbearance for the woman. After receiving her solemn promise to my request and the demands I had made on her, the legal transfer of the town property was completed.

During our parting good-byes, I explained that I was looking forward to my new adventures in Texas and that I also wished her happiness and success in her new adventure. We parted with shared hope that our friendship would continue and that we would continue to exchange letters in the future so we might share our thoughts and endeavors.

ooooo

The Texas Indian Policy of 1845 required the building and manning of several fort installations along the borders of the frontier. However, by 1850, the federal government had given up trying to move the Indians out of Texas. Instead, they opted to establish two reservations within the state, one near Fort Belknap and the other at a site on the Clear Fork branch of the Brazos River.

There was intense hatred building among Texas settlers against the Indians while the Indians had only vindictiveness and hate for the Texans and blamed them for their problems. This mutual hatred reached a high pitch with the Indian's persistent raids and brutality. Bands of Indian raiders stormed across the Red River into north Texas with frequency for looting and theft of horses, cattle, and mules.

With no concern for the Texas white settlers, the Indians continued with their savage ambush tactics bringing about the murder of men, women, and children, kidnapping others, and stealing or destroying their victims' property. Following these incursions, the crafty raiders would quickly retreat back across the river into Indian Territory for safety. Settlers' children were sometimes kidnapped and returned to Indian Territory to reside and become permanent residents or "white Indians"—never to be returned to their parents. On occasion, stolen cattle, mules and some kidnapped women and children were taken to Indian Territory where they could be used for trade or ransom.

Out of necessity in the early part of the Civil War, members of the U.S. Army's 2nd Cavalry was relieved of its command at the established forts in Texas and ordered to move from the state to more pressing engagements elsewhere. With the cavalry's sudden and unexpected departure, any and all semblance of frontier security vanished in Texas. Lawlessness and chaos followed and was soon raging everywhere. Settlers were left to defend for themselves by whatever means available. After the war out of necessity, several new forts were established at various locations within the state with a renewed effort for putting down the persistent Indian hostilities and uprisings.

Within the Texas Republic, the relatively small number of slave owners gradually gained control of the state's economy, its culture, and what proved most important, its politics. By 1850, the majority of the few Texas residents were residing in the north and eastern regions of the state. San Antonio had become the largest city at the time while Galveston, with its strategic shipping location on the Gulf of Mexico, had seen significant growth and had become the state's second largest city.

Most early settlers in Texas cultivated their land and began raising both cotton and corn. A few cows and hogs were frequently kept to supplement their diet. In 1857, a farm of 160 acres in Texas could be purchased for the total sum of $400. Commonly in the settler's family, the husband hand made his desired farm implements and household furniture. His wife sewed the family's clothing, made its soap, candles, and bedding. In stores and businesses located in scattered small settlements supplies and goods needed by these families, were purchased through negotiation and the customary barter system.

By 1860, slaves accounted for 30 percent of the Texas population. Most were laborers in the cotton fields and were owned by landholders who comprised the politically influential small group. By the beginning of the Civil War, the majority of Texas citizens claimed to be pro-Union while sympathizers for the South accounted for only 20 percent.

In February 1861, with strong political influence generated by the small number of slave owners, Texas seceded from the Union and joined with

South Carolina in the new Confederate government. The great disparity in political thinking, now obvious within the state, was certain to create future problems—and it did.

Then Texas governor Sam Houston was a slave owner. Politically however, he remained a staunch Unionist but also strongly favored state's rights. He declared his feelings openly to the state's citizens saying, "Secession is totally wrong for Texas!" More explicitly he added, "I fought for Texas, and I will not fight against her." Shortly after issuing his passionate statement, he left office.

Men from Texas provided varied rolls for the Confederacy during the war with well over 70,000 Texans serving in the Confederate army. Texas residents were engaged in some capacity in every major battle of the Civil War with all of them fighting against the Union. The state provided forty-five regiments of cavalry and twenty-three regiments of infantry. The state's forces sustained especially heavy losses in the horrific battles of Antietam (Sharpsburg) and Gettysburg.

The most notable battle occurring within the state's borders was fought on September 8, 1863, known as the Battle of Sabine Pass. Forty-six Texans defeated a Union force of nearly 4,000. The small group won victory by their superb gunnery tactics against the Union flotilla that numbered twenty-seven ships. With tenacity and grit, the Texans caused the Union navy to retreat towards New Orleans.

20

Just as Uncle Silas had experienced in Columbia, parting from my patients and friends in Sedalia was more difficult than I had ever imagined. On a spring day in 1875, I boarded the MK&T (Missouri-Kansas-Texas) train for my new venture into Texas. The Katy railroad, as it was called, had expanded and grown important following the war. In late 1872, the Katy finally made a connection into Denison, Texas, but at that time there was no expansion further west.

When boarding the Katy that day, I was filled with excitement about the opportunities and experiences I was anticipating in Texas. It was going to be another entirely new and different territory for me, but once again I was prepared for its challenges. I had heard numerous stories about Texas with its Indian problems. These stories came mostly from sick and injured trail drovers I had treated in Sedalia.

As the train began moving out of the Katy station, a tall, distinguished older gentleman took a seat across the aisle from me. He was meticulously well groomed. His white beard and hair suggested that he was considerably older in date than me. I was quickly enamored when noting his handsome crafted boots. I was suspicious of his being from Texas.

In a pleasant deep resonating voice he inquired, "Good day, my friend. I'm Conrad James. Where might ya be headin'?"

"Good day to you as well. After reaching Texas, my plans are somewhat uncertain. I'm a doctor and have plans to begin my practice in the state but haven't yet decided as to location. For the past ten years I've been practicing in Missouri, but now the Texas frontier is beckoning. My name's Somers Watson and glad to make your acquaintance, Mr. James."

I could tell the Texas gentleman had been studying me closely, after which he replied, "Oh please, just call me Conrad. I've been in Sedalia closin' out some cattle business. My home was originally in North Carolina. Several years before the damn war began, I took off for Texas and bought whatever number of acres of land I could afford at the time, and then began raisin' cattle.

As ya probably are aware, our Texas economy was in god-awful shape right after the war for a while. A few of us old ranchers have been fortunate to get that turned around, thanks to improved cattle prices. After General Lee surrendered, those Yankees up east decided they were starvin' for a good taste o' beef, so that's made a great difference for us down home."

Shifting in his seat and with pride showing on his weathered and tanned face, he continued, " I was fortunate to have bought up a fair piece of land in the beginnin' and have gradually added more acres over time whenever possible. But when the damn war hit, I almost lost my shirt 'n' everythin'. However, right after the war I met up with some other cattle folks, and we started runnin' longhorns north, and we're still doin' it today. My place is just a short piece south of the Red River in Montague County. It's a stone's throw from a special spot where we always send the cattle across the Red. With the great number of drives headed north these days, it's made our area a mighty well known place in the cattle business."

"Your story fascinates me. I'm originally one of those guys from out east—I'm originally from Philadelphia. I came to Missouri just out of medical school and practiced with my uncle a few years. Finally, some Jayhawkers murdered Uncle Silas after they found he had treated a severely injured black cattle drover."

Listening to my story and showing continued interest, Mr. James spoke with sincerity in his voice, "Doctor, I'm damn sorry to learn 'bout your uncle. I've heard plenty 'bout those guerilla wars takin' place up there. That whole slave deal and the war it caused wasn't good for anybody."

Conrad wiped a tear from his eye and then continued, "Thanks to several enterprising men a few years back, an important trail makes its way north only a short piece from my land. Mr. Jesse Chisholm was largely responsible for gittin' it forged all the way up to the big Abilene railhead. I had the honor of meetin' the good man a few times before he died. Folks say he died of food poisonin' and claimin' it was from eatin' rancid buffalo meat. I'm still not sure whether to believe that. Nevertheless, Jessie was a great man, and all of us down home must be thankful for what he done for us cowmen."

As our train continued down the track, my cowboy friend's stories filled me with intrigue and increased my eagerness to arrive in Texas. Judging by the gentleman's looks, the cattle business had treated him well.

"Please tell me more about the area where you live." By now I had become interested in hearing more about north Texas and if it might be an area that I might want to consider."

Conrad paused for a moment and then explained, "Fortunately, our state didn't experience the ravages of the war. In my area, it's always been what everybody has been callin' the frontier, however, with the cattle drives there has been increasing numbers of settlers and merchants comin' in. We've had more damn trouble with the Indians than any battles we mighta ever had between the North and the South. Since I never owned slaves, I never got too upset one way or the other.

Durin' the war, I stayed on my land and tried keepin' the damn Comanche raiders from stealin' my horses and cows. Me, Momma, and the three boys got along best we could. Our youngest boy, Johnny, went off to the war and never came back. Seems he was up there in that god-awful Gettysburg battle. Sure do miss that boy. His two brothers are still with me runnin' the ranch, thank goodness. Momma's been gone a few years now. Don't think she ever got over losin' her baby in that war. After Momma died, the boys and I have kept our place goin'. Now that I'm gettin' a little timeworn, I'm sure thankful my boys have stayed with me.

Ya see, Doc, at the close of the war, all the country west of a line between Eagle Pass an' Gainesville was really uncivilized with just a few folks livin' there. Every blasted ranch and village above that line was subject to them damn Indian raids, and you could almost bet there'd be a raid someplace on every full moon for sure. Even after the government built more forts across Texas, those cunning savages outwitted the soldiers time and again."

We heard the train's loud whistle indicating a stop just ahead for water. My new friend stopped talking for a time, and we both gazed out the window as the train rolled to a smooth stop.

"Are there any towns in your area?" I inquired. I could already see Mr. James had a kind heart and spoke his feelings. I also understood why he had tears moments before. Conrad and his family had truly suffered from the rages of the war by paying a very great price.

With the train taking on water, we both stood and stretched. Mr. James continued, "Since Texas became a state in 1845, there's been settlers comin' in to buy up farmin' land. Guess I already mentioned ol' Jesse Chisholm, but he played a big part in gittin' this part of the state goin'. His bein' part Cherokee Indian, he had a foreknowledge of the country and how to deal with the rest of those damn Indians and that proved damn important for everybody. My ol' friend, J. J. Myers sent one of the very first herds all the way up the Chisholm to Abilene. I've known the ol' colonel for some time and he was one hell of a drover, let me tell you!

The old Red River has been another stickin' point for us. There are times when monster rains hit, and that's when the ol' river can get pretty treacherous. Swimmin' the cattle across the Red at those times has been a real problem for us to contend. It's not safe for man or beast at those times. Sometimes we just have to wait for the Red to quiet down before we start movin' again.

There's one place where the Red makes a real sharp bend that changes the flow. That's been a natural crossin' for the cattle most all the time and there's no quicksand neither. Near that place to cross, a little community got started…known as Salt Creek. I've watched the whole area gittin' more settled all the time. It just might be a real good place for a young doctor like you to hang your hat."

After hearing the whistle, our train began moving again, and we were on our way. I began thinking about what he had said about the developing area along the river. It would be worth my inquiry.

I had every reason to believe Mr. James was well informed on the possibilities for a new doctor in his area. Once again my travel partner continued, "I must also tell you that Burlington's just a short distance east o' the crossing and less than a mile south. Several businesses have started up there includin' a general store, a blacksmith and livery stable, a hotel, and a damn saloon you wouldn't believe. It's called Schrock's Cowboy Saloon. Oh my goodness, Doc, that ol' J.W. has himself some kinda business in that saloon. Trouble is, it's become a gosh durn wild place! A few houses are also bein' built in the area. With the great numbers of cattle trailin' north, it's a good place for gatherin' up supplies and the like for all the outfits. When we get to Montague County, if you'd be in the favor, I'd be mighty happy to show you around."

"That would be most kind of you. I'd like to visit the whole area. It sounds like it might have need for a doctor."

The old cowboy smiled and said, "There hain't no doubt 'bout that, my friend. Ya see, runnin' those big, long-horned cows 'n' steers can be risky business since they are oftentimes damn wild. Doc, drovers are always gittin' hurt and need attention. Why, last year a young boy in my outfit drowned crossin' the Red. We didn't find him for almost two days. He was a good hand, and I sure hated to lose him. We also get some shootin's quite often. Seems some of those white deserters from the war became no good outlaws and hide out up in Indian Territory. They come down to our area for their supplies and end up raisin' hell in town."

ooooo

Our trip to Denison took much longer than I had expected. We made our usual stops for water along the way and special rest stops for meals and to stretch like in Joplin and then several stops through Indian Territory. Fortunately, we encountered no problems, and Mr. James and I were able to catch a few catnaps at different times along the way. All his stories had been so entertaining and informative. By the time the Katy finally arrived in Denison, Conrad James and I had developed an affable and warm friendship.

As we prepared to step off the train, my friend offered, "Dr. Watson, let's you and me share a coach ride on home to Montague County, and I can point out a few places I know something about along the way if I haven't already burdened you with my jabber."

It sounded like a great invitation. I had greatly enjoyed the kind man's company and was eager to learn even more. Without hesitation I responded to his offer, "Let's do just that."

Mr. James treated me to a dinner in Denison while they were moving my two trunks onto the stagecoach and the horses were being prepared to leave. I learned later the stage we were boarding normally only carried mail to Gainesville and a couple of communities beyond, but apparently Conrad had arranged with the coach company for the two of us to ride with the mail sacks. Mr. James warned we would have a rather bumpy ride of about seventy or so miles before reaching home with station stops along the way for fresh horses and mail exchange.

Somewhat apologetically he continued, "If I'm bein' tedious and you'd rather sleep than listen to an ol' cowboy regale his yarns, I beg you to address your concern and I'll put a stop to it."

"I'd be most grateful for you to continue since I have so much to learn." There was no way I could sleep and miss Conrad's stories.

The man then took on a more serious demeanor, saying, "Since you've never been down in my part of the world, I beg your indulgence since there are things for your own good you should know. Perhaps I might add a little council that an' old trapper like me can give that might help you. First and foremost, you have now arrived in a pretty hard-boiled area that you may have no custom. We still have some Indian raids, and in our area they steal every horse they can find. The cussed Indians have always stole horses in the past and then traded them back to white men. For that reason, if ya don't already have a pistol to carry, we need to fetch you one so you can keep it on you all the time.

You may recall me tellin' about that special site on the river where we move our cattle across. Well, before 1860, peaceful Indians lived and farmed the fertile bottomland in that area. White settlers moved in, and after the war, when the trail drives really got goin', that place became the 'jumpin' off' last stop in Texas 'fore gittin' yourself into that dangerous Indian Territory.

Thousands and thousands of longhorns arriving in the area from the south are usually allowed to rest for a day or two just south of the river when possible. There's around 350,000 head goin' across the Red nearly every year but the numbers vary from year to year. After gittin' supplies and their social life improved in Burlington, the drovers usually plan on movin' the cattle across to the north bank and into Indian Territory the followin' mornin'. Doctor, you won't believe your eyes when you see all those horned critters makin' their way across that river. It's quite a sight, even if I do say.

Soon's the herds are settled down, those guys are off to Burlington for a good time that night at the waterin' holes and with the ladies. I'll leave all that to your imagination. After days and weeks perched in that saddle, you can damn well bet they're ready for a night on the town."

My many memories going back when Uncle Silas and I first arrived in Sedalia fit precisely with Conrad's comments regarding Burlington, Texas. I was prepared with the exception of carrying a pistol, but I certainly would abide by the cowman's advice on the matter.

After arriving in northern Montague County, Conrad went out of his way to make me feel at home and made me a welcomed guest in his ranch home, where I was introduced to his two sons. Conrad spent considerable time showing me around the communities of Burlington and Salt Creek. We enjoyed several journeys through the countryside and viewed the Red River for some distance. I found it exactly like he'd described. It was a scenic area with its hills and valleys.

On the day of our arrival at Salt Creek, I had the opportunity to witness two consecutive drives crossing the river, and I can well recall what a sight it was for a city guy from Philadelphia. The excitement of it all gave me reason to make my decision to begin practice in Burlington. I could see its potential growth and the need for a doctor. I did not realize at the time how that decision would have such an important affect on my life.

My first purchase after arriving in Burlington was a small pistol, which I learned to carry with me at all times. After my decision was made to stay in Burlington, finding office space was an immediate problem. With Conrad's kindness and assistance, I was able to rent a small space alongside the hardware store. The quarters proved to be cramped and less refined from what I had left in Sedalia, but I chose to make do. My living quarters were in one of Burlington's boarding houses.

Everyone in the small community welcomed me from the beginning. Once I had my office and the boarding house living quarters arranged to my satisfaction, I began seeing patients. The date was May 5, 1875. The Texas area was so different from what I had experienced in Missouri. I was soon to learn that I had much to learn about Texas. Nevertheless, I was happy to be settled and ready for all its challenges, whatever they might be.

21

The Red River received its name from the heavy red soil sediment it often carried. While being the most southern of the primary branches of the Mississippi River it flows for about 1,300 miles with its drainage basin covering nearly 90,000 square miles.

Its origin is found in the Texas Panhandle with the source of its north fork east of Amarillo and the Prairie Dog Town fork rising to the south. Most of the Red's eastern course forms the interstate boundary between the states of Oklahoma and Texas. As the course of the river continues east, it flows through southwestern Arkansas and then into Louisiana where it joins with the Mississippi River about 340 miles from the delta.

ooooo

With their history dating back to the early 1700s, the Taovaya Indian tribe made their way into the Red River's fertile bottomlands. For protection, they lived in settlements where they constructed small grass-thatched dwellings. They began farming the surrounding rich bottomland for their sustenance.

The industrious and peaceful tribe began active trading with the French who were also dwelling in the area. In 1750, with fear of Spanish incursions developing along the river, the French built a small fort on the river's bank to defend against anticipated attacks whenever they might come.

In 1759, the anticipated attack did come from a Spanish regiment with ideas for taking over the entire river area in addition to the French fort. However, when the Taovaya and a band of Comanche combined forces, they soundly defeated the Spanish invaders in a battle lasting but four hours. The aggressive warlike Comanche Indians then routed what Spanish invaders remained alive some distance out of the Red River area to a San Saba mission. The battle was brief but of great importance historically since the Spanish never again attempted a march into America's heartland with conquest in mind.

Disaster befell the Taovaya tribe in 1778 when they were nearly decimated by more than one deadly scourge of small pox. With the tribe's numbers having become significantly reduced by the fatal disease, some headed west to merge with the Wichita tribe. Tragedy struck again when their remaining small group suffered from a vicious attack from a marauding band of the Osage Indian tribe. The small group of Taovayas was unable to defend themselves and later sought refuge by moving their remaining small settlement across onto the south bank of the river. By 1834, their number was reduced to fewer than 500. The small group precariously continued to survive on the south bank until immigrant white settlers began arriving between 1859 and 1860.

The few remaining Taovayas, were now outnumbered and unable to resist the white man's advances onto their land. Without choice and for their ultimate survival, they were compelled to relocate permanently inside Indian Territory. Meanwhile, white settlers continued moving into the area and confiscating the river bottomland.

Daniel Montague was a trained surveyor. He moved into Cooke County originally to engage in the survey of its borders. Later in 1857, he platted nearly 900 square miles of land in north central Texas that had the Red River as its northern boundary. The western Cross Timbers section of the recently formed Texas Republic was part of that survey. Its terrain consisted of level to gently rolling land and high rolling prairies with deep broad valleys. Montague became a prominent landowner and eventually a state senator. The county he surveyed and platted was later given his namesake.

In late 1861 just west of Salt Creek and near its mergence with the Red River, a crude outpost was constructed. By early 1862, a small frontier militia was garrisoned at the fort to protect the Republic's northernmost border from the frequent and troublesome Indian attacks upon the area's new settlers. The small militia proved no match when overrun more than once by much larger marauding bands of Indians swarming across the river.

To assist in providing food for their troops during this time period, the Confederate army requisitioned large numbers of Texas cattle that were running wild in Montague, Clay, Wise, and Jack counties. The few cowmen coming from those counties began their round-ups in the spring and fall. During that time of year, they lived in small shelters called line camps. The camps were crudely constructed from sod and timbers. but they did help in providing protection from the weather's elements as well as potential Indian attacks.

By 1864, the battle weary and beleaguered Confederacy found itself in desperate need of additional troops for several battles outside Texas. Out of necessity, the small Red River detachment garrisoned at the fort was quickly drafted into the regular Confederate army. It was moved out now leaving Montague County and the north Texas area totally unprotected from the constant threat of Indian raids. For their own added self-protection from those raids, the Texas cowmen abandoned their cow camps and occupied the vacant fort on the Red River.

Prior to and during the Civil War, no development of any significance took place within Daniel Montague's platted area. Between the war and the hostile Indians a temporary regression in growth and expansion of the western frontier resulted; the new county of Montague being no exception. Renegade white outlaws and bands of marauding Indians made their way across the Red with frequency storming into the area leaving its few white settlers in constant fear.

The Comanche and Kiowa tribes were especially troublesome. Historians have labeled the

Comanche tribe as the Lords of the plains. Comanche raids on the county settlers were frequently violent and brutal, although many raids were merely to steal horses. Surviving family accounts of this brutality remain on record. In the county's earliest days, the most valuable possessions a settler might have would be an exceptionally swift-footed horse and his gun.

When first knowledge would come of Indian presence in the area, a brave settler known by the neighbors as the Indian Runner, would mount his well known swift-footed horse and rush at full speed to warn as many neighbors as possible. The rider and his horse became the settlers' first line of defense.

Prospective settlers looked upon Texas as a place for a new beginning after their lives had been disrupted in many ways by the war. Land in Montague County at that time sold for as little as $3.00 an acre. New settlers arrived in the area riding on heavy ox-driven wagons filled with supplies. Accompanied by pack mules and horses, they often had already blazed their own lonely and dangerous trails across the prairie to reach their final destination.

Not until 1868 did significant growth and development begin taking place in Montague County. On a single day in early 1870, a train of over forty wagons with their large number of settlers and supplies arrived from Alabama. By that date, it's been said it was the largest migration at any one time into Texas. Most settlers arriving in the state from the north and east had traveled through Indian Territory or had come from New Orleans by way of the Gulf of Mexico, making their entrance into Texas at Galveston.

In June 1874, and with desperation, the Comanche, Kiowa, and southern Cheyenne tribes went to war. Their continuous and often time savage raids shook the entire South Plains. That war of attrition lasted one year due to the relentless pursuit of the Indians by the military. With the drastic decline in numbers of buffalo on the plains, attrition began to take its toll. The Indian raiders eventually began their surrender. Quanah Parker and his Kwahadi Comanche followers were the last to continue their struggle. They surrendered at Fort Sill in 1875. The Red River wars were virtually over.

ooooo

It's not known when the nomadic and crafty Indians occupying each side of the Red River first discovered the unique habit of the roaming buffalo herds. The Indians observed the buffalo always crossing the river at or near the very same location. Even following heavy rains in the area when the river's current became a treacherous torrent, the buffalo continued crossing precisely at the same location. Following the buffalos' habit, the Indians began crossing the river in the same locale.

That site was south of the Fleetwood Branch of the Red and just north of what would become Salt Creek. At that site the Red River made a sharp bend north which in turn forced the current of the river against the south bank. Its channel was also quite narrow at that location. Unlike other areas, the site was also free of the always treacherous quicksand. Crossing at that point proved safe and ideal for both man and beast.

Also of great importance, by their nature, the banks of the river at the Salt Creek location were exceptionally wide apart and of significant height. The ideal natural configuration forced the herds of cattle to be crowded or "funneled" into the narrow channel of the river.

ooooo

Fifty families had settled in the community of Salt Creek in northwest Montague County by 1866. Four years later, twelve blocks were surveyed and platted for business sites. With its location near the famous river crossing, the community began to prosper.

That year cattle drives became frequent with increased numbers and size of the herds. It was estimated 260,000 head were pushed across the river that year alone. With this expanding business enterprise coupled with the growing number of settlers entering the area, more than one community began appearing across the county's prairie grasslands.

In 1872, John Rich moved into the county and after purchasing 500 acres a mile south of the river, he platted another town which he named Burlington. Enterprising businessmen began arriving there as well. Construction began on several buildings, some two-story. A variety of new businesses developed in a short time and John Rich's town square had taken on the appearance of a growing and prosperous frontier town.

By 1874, Burlington could boast the presence of more than one hotel, multiple saloons, blacksmiths, a livery stable, hardware, drug and general mercantile stores, and a gristmill. Nearly 300 residents were living in Burlington a year later.

Cattle drives were creating major new business interest in the area, all adding to the county's growing economy. An amassed giant herd numbering in the tens of thousands (twenty documented smaller herds were part of the single massive herd) waited outside Salt Creek on one occasion for favorable weather conditions to begin crossing the river.

In the early 1870s, mail was being delivered to the north Texas area by the famous but short lived Pony Express. It was replaced by stagecoach transport out of Gainesville, Texas. In 1877, two years after my arrival, Burlington made an official request for obtaining its own federal post office, but their request was denied since Texas already had another community and post office by that name. For that reason, Burlington's name was changed to Spanish Fort. A new post office was then granted.

Cattle prices showed a marked and progressive increase between 1866 and 1870. In fact, 1871 was a banner year for the industry when over 700,000 head of longhorns were driven out of Texas. Most of that number crossed the river at Salt Creek and were then driven on to Midwestern and Eastern markets.

Unfortunately, the economics of the industry changed nearly over night. Supply and demand produced a precipitous drop in cattle prices after 1871. There was accompanied financial panic. By 1872, the herd numbers crossing the Red were reduced by half from the previous year. Numerous Texas cattlemen and some Eastern high-dollar cattle investors folded into bankruptcy, never returning again to the cattle business.

J. M. Grayson, a blacksmith and gunsmith in Salt Creek constructed a large house in 1872 two miles outside of town. Its lumber was transported by ox cart from Jefferson, Texas, by way of Sherman. The basement beneath Grayson's house served as a school and community meeting place for a time. Grayson and W.S. Thurston, also a blacksmith and owner of the hardware store, became exceptionally prosperous in Salt Creek. Thurston is said to have introduced the first coffin in town.

Salt Creek retained its name and post office until 1884 when it became known as Red River Station.

Saloons, a grocery store and "Molly Love's" hotel added to the economy and active "social life" for the small community.

Dynamic cultural changes brought about a colorful history for north Texas and the Montague County area between 1866 and 1888. Millions of cattle and thousands of transient cowboys crossed the "mighty Red" which helped create that history. Fear and excitement became commonplace on the streets of the two towns and inside their raucous and smoky saloons. Whenever headstrong individuals became mixed with guns and liquor, deadly encounters were sure to follow. Perhaps nowhere was this more evident than at J. W. Schrock's Cowboy Saloon in Spanish Fort.

Fights and brawls with fists and guns were the norm and most often following a drunken patron's snide remark, a spilled whiskey or an unpaid gambling debt. The walls of J.W.'s saloon over time became pockmarked from slugs fired from the guns of intoxicated and raucous patrons. Shootings and killings became an accepted part of community life. It's reported that on one Christmas morning three men had been murdered before breakfast.

Salt Creek community had likewise become a popular watering hole from time to time for such well known and notorious outlaw visitors as the James brothers- Jesse and Frank, Wes Hardin, Al Jennings, as well as the legendary "Bandit Queen," Belle Starr. These renegade Confederates were only a few of the people who had become embittered by the war's outcome and continued with their life of retaliation and crime. While passing through Texas, the Station was one place where they frequently stopped for a brief visit, a game of cards and whiskey cocktail, or hunting down someone who had done them bad.

As the railroads continued their expansion west, new railheads and communities began taking shape. New cattle trails found their way through towns like Ellsworth and Dodge City, Kansas, where new shipping yards and railheads had developed. With the arrival of the cattle and drovers, came raucous excitement in each new town. With new trails and shipping sites for cattle, the town of Abilene with its massive shipping yard began to lose the importance it once had enjoyed.

ooooo

Several sites along the Red River became important and popular ferry crossings for wagons, people, and goods between north central Texas and the Indian Territory. As early as the 1850s, the Chickasaw Nation had created and operated ferry crossings resulting in increased trade between the Territory and Texas.

The federal mail carried by the Butterfield Stagecoach Company routinely crossed at Colbert's Crossing operated by a Chickasaw tribal member. Over the years, bridges were constructed at some of these crossing sites, but the majority, at some time or other, were swept away with torrential floods and never rebuilt. A short distance upstream from Red River Station, an active ferry crossing was located and used with great frequency.

By the year 1887, cattle drives were beginning to lose their importance and the Chisholm Trail had become almost shut down and was soon to become just a memory for what it once had been. For nearly two exciting and very important decades the Station's ideal location on the famous Red River had been the drovers' major point of entry and exit for the Indian Territory. The small raucous communities in northern Montague County Texas had provided the cattle industry a place to purchase supplies, make necessary repairs, have a whiskey or two, and be pleasured by a lady.

It is conservatively estimated that well over 4,000,000 head of cattle crossed at or near Red River Station during the dynasty of the trail drives. Whether it was the thundering and pounding hooves of thousands of longhorn cattle, the loud rumbling and thunder associated with violent rainstorms, or the alarming and often deadly blasts from guns; all were part of what helped make history for two very small frontier Texas communities—namely Spanish Fort and Red River Station. In the years following the cattle drives, one community gradually decayed to a point of becoming a virtual ghost town while the other slowly returned to nothing but dirt and prairie grass. But most important, each community will always retain its rightful place in the pages of history.

22

The dynamic importance the cattle industry had on the colorful history of the western frontier can never be overemphasized. Its importance remained small scale during the earliest years of the Texas Republic. During that time, the economic value placed on cattle was primarily derived from their hides and little else. The hides were destined for use in the growing leather industry; however, that changed dramatically after 1850 when the longhorn's value increased sharply due to a special need for meat on the country's west coast.

The first organized cattle drives in America were begun to supply meat for the growing number of gold prospectors arriving in California to seek their fortune. At that time an adult longhorn steer's value in Texas averaged between $5.00 and $10.00 per head, whereas in San Francisco the same animal's value had reached $50.00 to $100.00.

The economics was evident providing the cattle could be moved successfully the long distance to California. The first drives had their origins near San Antonio and were trailed through El Paso and then on to either San Diego or Los Angeles and then finally reaching San Francisco. Five to six months was required to make such a trip, providing there was good going along the way.

All great fortunes at some time come to an end. By 1857, a giant surplus of cattle had reached San Francisco resulting in a much softer market. After that year and during the Civil War, the wane taking place throughout the country and especially the entire western frontier brought cause for cattle ranching in Texas to a point of near total collapse. After war's end in 1865, people in the North had grown hungry for beef. They had good fortune! Massive numbers of longhorn cattle were running wild in Texas and were readily available to meet that need, providing they could reach the mid west and eastern states. Within one year, the cattle ranching industry became revitalized in Texas and was quickly becoming stronger than before. The lonely cattle drover had once again found his niche in history.

The cattle drover or cowboy of those years was a very special breed. Few had an education and most were quite independent, but after joining an outfit would become fervently loyal. Physically, most were of slight to medium build and wiry (heavy men were hard on horses). Many of these young men possessed hot tempers that fit well with their personalities, often wild and reckless. Most were never shy in making their feelings known. This trait often created problems for them. Whenever and wherever trouble was brewing, a drover was likely found in the middle.

The revitalized cattle drives following the war established an entirely new profession of cowmen—the trailing contractor. Enterprising Texas cattlemen foresaw the promising opportunity to make money once again. The enterprising self-imposed contractor hired the men he wanted for his outfit and then assumed final responsibility for the herd's successful arrival to the chosen railhead wherever that might be. Typically, the contractor received $1.00 to $1.50 per head for each trip he organized and completed.

The group composing a contractor's outfit and on his payroll would usually consist of ten to fifteen men. Two-thirds would likely be Caucasian while the remaining members would be Hispanic or black, but on rare occasion, an Indian. The usual outfit was composed largely of older teens and men in their early to mid 20s.

The trail boss (ram rods) was likely to be Caucasian, but somewhat older in age. Their usual salary might range up to $125.00 per month. The wrangler, perhaps somewhat older and more mature, received a salary of $30.00 per month. He had full responsibility for the remuda that would usually consist of at least eight to ten horses per man. Mature and older cooks typically received $60.00. All others, often referred to as waddies or "thirty-dollar men, received a monthly salary of $30.00.

The cook's meals were simple, monotonous and nutritionally poor. His typical menu might include beef or bison steak or a stew prepared from assorted calf parts, bacon (called "chuck wagon chicken"), beans ("pecos strawberries"), biscuits ("sourdough bullets"), and strong coffee.

Although the drover's salaries were meager, lack of sleep always seemed their greatest complaint when out on the trail. They tolerated the poor menu despite their frequent complaints, rarely bathed, and conditions often required their sleeping on cold hard ground in dirty wet clothing. Amenities did not exist for the drover on the trail.

Cattle were customarily driven eight to fifteen miles each day with a planned one- or two-day rest each week. Moving across a lengthy dry stretch of country presented its own unique problems. On those occasions, the cattle were commonly driven throughout the day and most of the following night before resting in the early predawn hours when the air had cooled.

During the burning hot daylight hours, it would not be uncommon to witness profuse drooling of saliva coming from the mouths of the cattle. In hot dry areas the enormous cloud of dust created by the massive herd might hang in the heavy air for miles. Cattle, when in such dry country, possessed nature's inherent ability to smell water several miles distant. Should that occur, sudden stampedes were a distinct possibility.

Under normal conditions, when the herd was approaching a body of water, the lead animals were deliberately forced to align themselves along the bank of the river facing downstream. The remainder of the herd and the drags would then have clear water when positioned along the bank much further upstream.

Stampedes were feared most; more so than any other peril on the trail. Those occurring at night during a thunderstorm were especially dangerous for the cattle and the drovers alike. When a stampede began for whatever reason, drovers up front got positioned as quickly as possible so as to begin milling the lead cattle into an ever-tightening circle. As more and more cattle were progressively pushed tighter and tighter together into the ever-widening circle, it forced the lead animals to be crowded so tightly in the center so as to slow and then cease their movement.

Typically, the youngest or new "add-on" drovers were assigned to ride the lonely "drag" position at the very rear of the herd where the dust cloud always proved to be the greatest and most annoying. Any drover being disciplined by the trail boss frequently found himself back there as well.

Herds were normally bedded down at night near the outfit's campsite. For security reasons, guard detail was employed throughout the night hours. Security was required and maintained primarily to help prevent theft of both cattle and the horses within the remuda. Two drovers on horseback worked a two-hour shift. Their task was to slowly circle the herd traveling in opposite directions until they met again on the opposite side. That maneuver would continue until their shift was completed and were relieved by two men for the following shift. The drovers found that humming or singing would quiet any restless animals.

ooooo

In 1865, several of the pre-existing railheads became likely destinations for cattle drives headed north. Unfortunately, there were few well-established and safe trails. Trails heading north and northeast required passage through the perilous Indian Territory. The Shawnee Trail was one such early trail. It began in south Texas progressing north to Waco, where it took a more northeasterly course up to the railhead in Sedalia, Missouri. Once in Sedalia, the Missouri–Pacific railroad moved the cattle to markets like Chicago and Kansas City.

The Shawnee had its problems too. In southwestern Missouri the heavily wooded and hilly terrain created problems in keeping the large herds together without their becoming separated and lost. Further problems came from hostile and angry farmers in the area, perhaps for good reason.

Few established trails became more utilized and better established than the Chisholm Trail. It was fortuitous for young Jesse Chisholm when he and his Cherokee Indian mother were left alone without a father and husband. Jesse's mother chose to return to the Indian Territory with her young son so they might live in her Cherokee Nation. With that fortuitous move, the boy was able to learn about Indian culture and have the opportunity to learn and speak several Indian languages. This knowledge proved extremely advantageous for him later in life.

His Indian education included necessities for personal survival and ways for exploring the expanse of the western plains. When a young man, Jesse became a knowledgeable and trustworthy guide with natural ability for conversing with the Indian and white man alike. His character and well-known reputation for trust and honesty followed him wherever he went. He established a very successful trading business and eventually built several trading posts across the frontier.

In 1864, with his wagons loaded with buffalo hides and supplies for sale or trade, Jesse followed a trail that had been blazed originally by a tribal Delaware Indian known as Black Beaver. This trail led Jesse through Indian Territory but some distance west of the troublesome Shawnee Trail.

This new trail was found to be relatively safe for travel. Initially, it was referred to by several names, but later received the official name of Chisholm Trail. Ironically, historical records fail to show any documented evidence that Jesse was ever involved with driving a single longhorn up the trail that was destined to become so famous and receive his name.

Soon after the war, Joseph McCoy, an ambitious and astute Illinois businessman recognized potential for personal wealth from cattle drives. He devised an elaborate plan for Abilene, Kansas. At that time, it was a small community with a railhead already present. His plan was to create a cattle-receiving depot or stockyard to expedite the handling of cattle coming off the trail to the Kansas-Pacific Railroad in Abilene for shipment to distant markets. After persuading the state's governor and the railroad of his plan, it was accepted. The railroad promised McCoy $5.00 per train carload of cattle that would ship from Abilene.

With personal and borrowed money, Joe McCoy purchased 250 acres nearby to the rail yard. He constructed a huge configuration of adjoining cattle pens. To provide relaxation and comfort for the tired drovers he also had constructed "The Drovers'

Cottage" a comfortable hotel with 100 rooms. Always looking to the future, McCoy added a bank on his property. By 1867, with the Chisholm Trail becoming extremely active, McCoy's yard and the town of Abilene were prospering. From its origin in South Texas the new trail stretched a distance of 500 miles to McCoy's pens in Abilene.

But before long, homesteaders living near the trail found the Texans and their longhorn cattle nothing but trouble. It was customary for farmers to keep a few head of domesticated European cattle on their property. The farmers' cattle began showing evidence of having acquired the dreadful "tic disease". It was learned the Texas longhorns, already having their own immunity from the disease, were guilty of carrying the disease up the trail and infecting the homesteaders' cattle.

With progressively more and more Texas cattle being moved north, tic disease became an urgent and significant problem for everyone including the federal government. Angry and spiteful farmers were known on occasion to deliberately stampede longhorn herds. They developed increasing hatred not just for the cattle but for the Texas drovers as well. At times, the problem erupted into bloodshed and a murder of some drover.

Finally, in response to the ever-growing problem, the federal government established and drew its initial quarantine line in 1872 south out of Abilene restricting longhorns from the area. McCoy's financially successful enterprise was forced to move its operation beyond the line, hence further west to Wichita, Kansas's new railhead. A stockyard was constructed there. However in 1876, a second quarantine line was created that forced the drives even further west. Trails were made into Dodge City and then continued north into Cheyenne, Wyoming. Along these new trails, small rough and raucous communities the likes of Ellsworth, Kansas, developed. To preserve law and order within those towns, peacekeeper lawman such as Wyatt Earp and Bill Hickock were hired to bring and maintain some type of order.

When the final amassed single herd of longhorns was brought together between April 1st and May 15th, each of the animals received an identical firebrand for the trail drive. Typical drives most often consisted of 2,000 to 10,000 head of cattle accompanied by the remuda and supply wagons. Since most drives out of Texas required four to six months to reach various railheads, whenever possible, they were scheduled so as to arrive at their respective destination before cold weather had set in. The contractor issued his designated trail boss either cash or a letter of credit for use while on the trail. On occasion the contractor might accompany the herd, but more often he would meet the herd upon its arrival at the railhead.

Surreptitious imbibing of alcohol by some individuals while on the trail and in the camps was common despite its prohibited use by most trail bosses. Most of the cowboy's carousing occurred in the frontier town's saloons. Reckless drunken cowboys were known to shoot out the saloon's lights or create property damage during a brawl. Although relatively rare, when gunfights did take place, it was usually for revenge or related to some misunderstanding. The trail boss would customarily compensate the saloon's proprietor for any damages incurred by his men the night before.

While on the trail, life was a lonesome, uncomfortable, and dangerous job, but it was one that many adventuresome teens and young men found to their liking. While some might only endure but one trip, others were eager to discover what new experiences the next drive might offer them.

The loneliness brought a need for social contact with women that were always available in brothels.

It must be remembered most drovers were healthy young individuals with a need and desire to show their sexual prowess. Each town's women of the night, being of all ages, were usually the type who enjoyed their chosen profession. Few would admit having any interest in marriage since that would require working daylight till dark in caring for family and home. But for others, prostitution's financial rewards were the lady's only means for her personal survival. Payment for their services varied as to amount, but for most women it was usually quite good!

The majority of prostitutes always seemed to have money, and quite often would make loans to their better-known clients to cover his gambling debt. Ironically, most of those loans were repaid.

23

I have many memories of my practice years in Montague County. From the beginning, I detected some constant fear of possible Indian raids still present among folks living in the distant and isolated rural areas. Such raids were always still a threat. A vicious deadly attack on the families of settlers was never more disturbing to me than the one that took the life of a close friend, John Fuller.

In the mid-hours of a warm and still summer night a full moon was casting its light through a few scattered clouds and across the landscape. The Fuller family's cabin was nestled in a clearing bordered by a dense group of oak trees. Inside, members of the family were sleeping. Like most other Montague County settlers, they had always remained fretful on such nights and with good reason.

Nights with a full moon were the favored times when Indian raids occurred with greatest frequency. It was a time when stealing horses and other livestock, kidnapping white women and children, or the butchering of white males in the family occurred too often. Most attacks usually came from small bands of Comanche or Kiowa warriors who had crossed the Red River earlier that evening and then stealthily made their way further south inside the county.

My friend John was a thirty-five-year-old Englishman, and like everyone, always feared such nights. Nights of the full moon always brought nothing but a fitful sleep for him. His pistol was routinely kept within easy reach next to his pillow. The .36-caliber Navy Colt with its pearl handgrips had come home on his person from Vicksburg where he had served with Lt. Gen. John Pemberton's troops. Arriving back home in Texas, John proudly acclaimed more than once to his friends that the weapon had saved his life on several occasions while in Virginia.

Sharla, his lovely wife, lay asleep beside her husband. It had been a long and exhausting day for her working in the family's large garden. The teenage son and daughter and their younger sister, were sleeping soundly in their beds at the far end of the cabin.

Outside, eight Comanche warriors waited in silence while seated on their ponies and partially hidden behind tall brush. Each was armed with either a carbine rifle or pistol. Three carried bone-head tomahawks while the others had carved stone daggers secured at their waist.

In preparation for their assault, Darkened Big Cloud, their dauntless and cunning leader, whispered final instructions and flashed hand signals to his group. They had already made plans for stealing the two horses and mule they had found inside the Fuller's barn nearby.

Darkened Big Cloud dismounted and then removed his rifle from its scabbard. He quickly made his way on foot to the cabin's front door. Another assailant jumped from his mount and rushed to his assigned post at the rear of the dwelling.

Using the butt of his rifle, Big Cloud pounded loudly several times on the door. The once quiet and tranquil night suddenly was disrupted with the frenzied war cries of the other warriors who had dismounted and invaded the cabin. Once the inflamed warriors had rushed inside, a vicious attack began on each family member.

Moonlight that was streaming inside the cabin thru the opened cabin doors and window created ghost-like shadows being violently jostled from place to place during the assault. In desperation, John was able to get off two shots, one of which struck and wounded one of the villainous invaders. Before he could fire additional shots, he was viciously subdued by two of the Comanche. Within a dreadful few moments, all of the family members had been brought into subjection.

Donna Jean, the teenaged daughter, courageously attempted to free herself from the grasp of the Comanche that had attacked her in bed. He responded to her attempt to escape by beating her head repeatedly with the butt of his pistol until she lost consciousness and fell limp onto the cabin floor. Believing her to be dead, the Comanche left her lying there and rushed outside.

Screaming and kicking at her abductor, Mrs. Fuller was forcefully dragged outside into the moonlit yard. The youngest daughter had been easily subdued and, like her mother, was dragged from the cabin. Big Cloud's warriors continued grappling with the terrified mother and her young daughter until each had their arms and legs bound

tightly together with the Indian's strips of buffalo hide.

Despite her continued but futile efforts to
escape, Sharla Fuller continued screaming at the
savage men. Two Comanche draped her bound
body across the back of one of their horses. Emily,
now bound like her mother, was likewise positioned across the back of an Indian pony.

Sharla continued her horrified and angry
screams at the warrior standing beside her.
Without warning, he suddenly pulled a dagger
from his waistband and placed its razor-sharp
stone blade against the woman's throat while issuing a maddening scream directed at the terrified
mother. Fearful of his next move, she quieted her
hopeless struggle.

While mayhem was taking place outside the
cabin, Darkened Big Cloud and two of his warriors had finally wrestled the boy and his father
outside and onto the cabin's front stoop. Each was
securely bound like the others. By now, Big Cloud
was incensed over having one of his men wounded
by John's pistol. Retaliation was in order, and when
the father and his son had been positioned in plain
view of Mrs. Fuller and Emily, the helpless father
and his fourteen-year-old son, Bill were severely

beaten then scalped alive. Their deadly screams pierced the night air followed by their final moans of agony—and then there was silence except for Sharla's sobbing.

Following the brutal and ghastly scalping deed one following the other, John and Bill's now lifeless bodies were bludgeoned with blunt-stone tomahawks until Big Cloud was convinced of their being dead. Crying and screams erupted again when Emily and her mother witnessed their two scalps being brazenly attached on the wall above the cabin doorway. John and Bill's deceased and mutilated bodies were left lying in the yard for hungry vultures to find after sunrise.

The wounded Comanche was helped up onto his pony while his barbarous comrades remounted with their horror-stricken female captives. After absconding the Fuller's horses and mule, the savage group departed from the repulsive scene. The night's full moon had become less brilliant and remained partially hidden by a larger storm cloud passing across the sky. Upon reaching the front road, the troop turned north for their return to their safe haven just across the Red River.

With the first rays of the early morning dawn being cast upon the horrendous scene, Donna Jean dazed and bleeding, regained consciousness. There was a deathly silence. The chaotic screaming and violence had ceased. Confused and with effort, she slowly and painfully gained her feet. She discovered herself to be alone with the deadly silence and grizzly scene and fate of her family members evident.

I was shocked beyond belief that morning when I got word about my friend's murder and his family's kidnapping and the brutal attack on Donna Jean during that night. Assisted by two family friends in town, I hurried out to the Fuller farm. We found John and Bill's mutilated bodies and buried each side by side in a vacant field near the cabin. We brought Donna Jean, stunned and filled with grief, to my office for treatment of her wounds. She described to me some details of the vicious attack. We never heard more concerning either Sharla or Emily. We could only assume they were destined to become "white Comanche".

ooooo

It was high noon when Cookie was about to ring the dinner bell and begin serving his prepared meal to the outfit's first shift of drovers. The cook's diminutive physical stature belied his gruff deep commanding voice. Although he took backtalk from no one, his small build gained the respect from every drover and discouraged even the most raucous drunkard from bringing him physical harm. In Cookie's stubborn mind, there was never an argument with anyone that he did not win. Over the years, he had served his beans and hard tack to many a hungry drover and not one had ever rendered him a complaint.

Somewhere inside Indian Territory on that mid summer day, danger lurked for Cookie and his fellow drovers. The chuck wagon and its supply wagon had established their position earlier that morning in preparation for the noon meal and brief rest period. By noon, several of the lead steers of the nearly 1,400 head had caught up with Cookie and his wagons and continued grazing nearby. Unbeknownst to Cookie, several of the longhorns when sensing a disturbance arising at the rear of the long trailing herd, suddenly made an unexpected break. Within moments, they were joined by a thundering stampede of several hundred animals. Many of the trailing herd began to scatter while others charged forward. The old seasoned drover and cook knew immediately a stampede was underway. He was perplexed since a stampede at mid day was most unlikely in Cookie's experience.

As far as one could see, cattle were running and scattering in every direction across the sun-parched prairie. An enormous deep rumbling sound was resonating with a swelling cloud of dust. With the massive number of pounding hooves striking the baked-hard turf, one could sense the ground shaking beneath their feet as if an earthquake had suddenly occurred. The dust cloud continued to build in size and density. It rose higher and higher into the air and began to shut out the sun as if night had suddenly descended across the desolate plains.

Another seasoned drover while riding left flank also quickly realized the problem at hand. Pushing his spurs deep and loosening his draw on the buckskin's reins, he sent his mount into full gallop hoping to gain distance on the herd so as to force several of the lead steers into the customary milling pattern.

Moving at breakneck speed, the drover and his horse were suddenly blinded by a crosswind of gale-like strength blowing sand and dust directly across their path from right to left. The cowboy lost complete vision and orientation, and without benefit of forewarning, he and his large mare hurled over a precipice of a forty-foot cut bank and tumbled violently down its side. Horse and rider came to rest atop several large sandstone boulders and brush covering the floor of the ravine.

Several hours later, the stampede was finally brought under control with the cattle quieted once again. Hiram Green, the outfit's trail boss, remained baffled. When taking a head count of his men, he discovered one missing. It was Harley Bridges, one of the outfit's most seasoned and dependable hands. At sun-up that morning, Hiram had assigned Harley to ride left flank.

A search party was dispatched immediately from camp to locate Harley. Everyone remained puzzled by the drover's unexplained absence. Before sundown, the weary search party came across the missing drover and his buckskin mare trapped at the bottom of the deep ravine.

Harley's lifeless body was found lying atop a huge sandstone boulder. His leg was twisted in a grotesque manner. His boot's spur had hung-up in the stirrup during the deadly fall. As search party members descended the steep bank, the badly injured buckskin mare raised her head in concerned recognition of their presence. She responded with a loud whinny and made repeated but unsuccessful attempts to free her hip and broken leg from between two large boulders. The drovers became emotionally distraught upon viewing the scene.

After removing their friend's lifeless body from the ravine, two of the saddened drovers wrapped him in their saddle blankets and buried it in a shallow grave nearby. They completed their task by gathering and placing several rocks atop the fresh grave to discourage wild animals from disturbing their friend's final resting place.

The sun was sinking low in the western sky when Hiram cautiously made his way once again down to the floor of the ravine. With tears welling in his eyes, Hiram withdrew his pistol and with two consecutive thundering shots, put an end to Dolly's life. Hiram and a drover removed the saddle and headstall from the dead cow pony.

The cow camp's evening fire was a beacon for the search party's sad and weary return without their friend as darkness had descended across the prairie. When later seated around the campfire eating the leftovers from supper, Hiram and his tired companions learned what had provoked the deadly stampede.

An inexperienced fifteen-year-old new hand had been one of three men riding drag. While sleepily riding along behind the trailing steers in the herd, the boy's horse was spooked by a large coiled rattle-snake. Being inexperienced, the young drover drew his pistol and fired two shots at the snake. The loud report of his gun startled a group of steers moving nearby causing them to begin their deadly run.

ooooo

While we were on the train traveling to Texas from Sedalia, I will not forget the comments Conrad James's made regarding his intense disgust and anger regarding the Indian raids occurring in Montague County. After my living in the county for a short time, I also shared his feelings. Bodily injury or occasional kidnapping of females and children had continued in our area but less often of late. Theft of horses remained a problem but raids seemed to be coming under control to my relief. Nevertheless, residents in our area continued living with varied degrees of fear each day. I was aware the government's military was finally getting some control of the problem.

When new homesteaders made plans for their cabin, whenever possible, the site was chosen as close to a fresh water source as possible. It was also customary for the wife and mother to have a designated area near the cabin for doing the family's laundry.

Harry Locker's homestead was only two miles south and east of Spanish Fort, just off a main road that the stagecoach traveled daily on its mail run from Gainesville to Head of Elm (later known as Saint Jo). On a late afternoon, while Harry labored in his cotton field, two Kiowa warriors ambushed Mrs. Locker with cunning deception and speed. She was alone and about to finish her laundry. They carried away the embattled woman amid screams and unholy dread of what was to come. Sadly, the woman was never seen nor heard from again.

ooooo

After completed construction of the transcontinental railroad in 1869, the expanding leather industry in America had created a profitable new business—the commercial buffalo hunter. Shipment of hides to the east by rail now became far more economical than formally accomplished by ox-driven wagons. While the industry was developing new methods for tanning leather, buffalo hides were becoming markedly more valuable.

Between 1870 and 1883, an unfortunate tragedy of greatest historic import took place across the frontier. During that time, the American buffalo became near complete extermination. This brazen sequence of events resulted from the acts of self-minded individuals with some personal greed, but primarily for business reasons. The economics for this new and growing profession was evident. The self-imposed hunter received $1.25 or more per buffalo hide. With such easy money to be made, the hunter and his assistant (the skinner) gave little thought to killing fifty to seventy-five animals daily. An additional twenty-five cents was received for each buffalo tongue.

With little, if any, personal regard for the roaming beasts, the hunters intentionally left the majority of the skinned carcasses to rot wherever the animal had fallen. During the same time, the number of buffalo being killed by the Indians for their sustenance was having no effect on the rapidly declining number of the large, shaggy animals across the frontier.

William Cody, better known as "Buffalo Bill", admitted at one time that he was personally responsible for killing nearly 10,000 buffalo. Other well-known hunters like Cody, boasted to similar numbers.

Meanwhile, the fate of the buffalo was affected also by the US Army becoming convinced that elimination of the buffalo would eventually bring about the final demise of a great majority of the hated plains Indians. It was those Indians who had become one of the Army's major problems following the Civil War. To make the problem worse for the buffalo and for reasons unknown, Congress showed little concern for the entire buffalo matter. Neither the rapid demise of the buffalo nor the Indian's need for survival gave members of Congress reason for taking any serious action. There was silent trust that with continued systematic killing of the buffalo it would eventually starve the troublesome Indian into submission.

Problems worsened with time. Increased disharmony developed between the Indian and the white man when after slaughtering the buffalo, the professional hunters began deliberately pouring coal oil over the freshly killed carcass. Now when finding a freshly skinned dead animal, the

Indian was maliciously prohibited from using it for food. The Indians continued their desperate pleas to save the animals since their very existence depended on the beasts, but their voice continued to fall on deaf ears in Washington.

Shelter, clothing, food, bedding, and numerous other items in addition to food came from the poor buffalo, the animal for which the Indian held out so much respect. Warriors of the Comanche tribe frequently carried a loosely slung shield made from a dried buffalo hide. They had discovered that once stretched into the shape of a shield, the hide proved strong enough to deflect a white man's rifle bullet.

The government did recognize and had assurance in knowing that wherever the large beasts roamed on the prairie, they were sure to be followed close behind by the savage Indian, thus exposing his location. The buffalo had little or no sense to run after anyone's initial shot had been fired. The lumbering beast, never swift of gait or alert to danger, became easy prey whether from the commercial hunter's rifle or the Indian's arrow.

Texas ranchers also had found favor for the buffalo's slaughter since it was not only limiting the Indian's food supply, but it also meant the buffalo was not competing with their range cattle for valuable and often times scarce prairie grass. However, the ranchers' false impression on this matter resulted with increasing numbers of violent Indian hostilities against the cowmen by Kiowa and Comanche tribesmen in north Texas.

By 1875, the flamboyant Colonel Randal Mackenzie of Civil War fame along with his raiders had subsequently driven most of the Comanche tribe from the plains and onto the reservation. By 1882, with the buffalo now virtually exterminated, the once profitable business of commercial hunting also had its demise.

The marauding Apache all this time were much like a sly and wary pack of wolves while harassing settlers and travelers. They lived in various camps scattered across the plains. Following their guerilla type raids, success for them was measured only by glory they brought for themselves and the amount of booty. Leadership within their groups came only from those individuals that had assumed personal dominance. Led by such brave warriors as Cochise, they were not only difficult for government troops to locate, but difficult to eliminate.

By 1885, government troops were finally successful in capturing the notorious and probably best-known Apache chief, Geronimo. His capture brought a virtual end to Indian hostilities in Texas. For history's sake, whether right or wrong, America had finally dominated the Native American tribes. The sad and bloody period in history had finally come to its end, but with a very great price.

After the plains tribes had been killed or forced onto the reservations and the buffalo had become nearly non-existent, there was a profound resurgence of cattle ranches, especially in Texas. Most of them were stocked with Texas longhorn cattle and managed by Texas natives. Meanwhile, immigrant settlers in great numbers continued making their way into the state.

24

After beginning my work in Texas, I found myself treating a considerable number of sick and injured transient cowboys that were passing through our area and across the Red River. Their injuries resulted from many different causes. It was not uncommon for a drunken cowboy and a local resident to become embroiled first in an argument, followed soon after with a brawl or rare shooting. When treating some of the more serious injuries, I called upon what skills I had learned from Uncle Silas years before.

Tadi Penan's story comes to mind. Tadi was a sixteen-year old Comanche who had originally come from Indian Territory. He was one of those rare Indian drovers that passed through town from time to time. The boy had been seriously injured shortly before his outfit arrived at the Red River. His trail boss brought him to my office for treatment and informed me that despite his young age,

Tadi was found to be an excellent horseman and capable wrangler in handling the outfit's remuda of over sixty-five horses.

The lad's name in Numinu, the Comanche language, meant Breezy Wind and Honey Hunter. He was slight of build but well muscled, strong, and wiry for his size. The trail boss mentioned that the boy could "take the buck" out of any rank horse. Having had a white Indian mother permitted us to communicate quite well.

The boy's story actually began in the fall of 1872 when the Army's MacKenzie and his raiders were issued orders to make a surprise attack on a large encampment of Comanche tribesmen. Their orders were to kill whatever number of men possible and to capture the women and children. The army's plan called for placing the captured women and children into prison for several months, then use them for ransom to obtain the co-operation and hopeful surrender of additional Comanche men. They had confidence this could be accomplished and the ransom would also entice other previously reunited families to peacefully surrender themselves onto the reservation.

During the attack, about twenty of the Comanche men were killed while over 100 women and children were captured and then transported on wagons to Fort Concho in west central Texas. The fort had been established in 1867 with an attached army garrison to provide protection for wagon trains of settlers as well as the stagecoach line transporting both passengers and mail across the west Texas plains. The fort's surrounding flat terrain permitted ideal visual surveillance for miles in all directions.

During the raid, the boy and his mother were made captives. Soon after the army wagons arrived at Fort Concho, Tadi's mother became gravely ill and died a week or so later. Tadi's father, a half-breed Comanche, was one of those killed in the raid. From his first day at the fort, the boy began making plans for his eventual escape. He wanted revenge for what had happened to his father and his mother.

Tadi's plan was to steal one of the garrison's horses from the stable and make his escape some night's late hour. For several days and evenings, he kept careful watch both on the stable and on the army private who was routinely assigned for night guard of the horses. The same soldier always appeared at his assigned post each night. Tadi discovered also that he would begin drinking from his concealed bottle of whiskey each night shortly after darkness once settled over the area.

Tadi began saving food from each of his meals to take with him on the night of his escape. After finding a slender long piece of sandstone, he began chipping off small pieces with meticulous care while shaping it into a sharp dagger.

In the darkness of the night he had chosen for his escape, with his sack of food and dagger, the Comanche lad hid near the stable making careful watch on the soldier. The private was armed as usual with his rifle and holstered revolver. On this night he had assumed his customary position sitting atop a cargo box. But on this night, he appeared asleep while his empty whiskey bottle was evident lying on the ground near his feet. Stealthily, the young Indian approached the sleeping soldier and, with a mighty thrust, plunged his crafted stone dagger deep into the drunken man's chest.

Moments later, now attired in the dead soldier's blood stained military blouse and the military kepi which he had placed smartly upon his own head, Tadi made his way over to the stable. Quietly and with due caution, he untied one of the horses. Grabbing his sack of food and the sentry's rifle and revolver, Tadi mounted and disappeared swiftly into the dark night. A few thin clouds partially hid the otherwise bright moon.

After riding a mile or so from the fort and feeling quite safe, he brought his stolen horse to a halt in an open field. The night sky, being almost cloudless, was perfect for viewing the heavens with its constellations of stars. After making a careful study of them, he made his decision and headed in an eastern direction.

From the story I was told, Tadi made it safely to Waco, Texas several days later. With his desire to return to his people in Indian Territory, he finally sought employment as a wrangler on one of the cattle outfits preparing to leave Waco and head north. The herd had already been assembled and branded when Tadi arrived and was hired. With the herd being trailed through Fort Worth, across the Red River, and then into Indian Territory, he was sure it would take him back to his people. Once inside Indian Territory, he would break away to rejoin the Comanche nation. The trail boss placed the boy on his payroll at $40.00 a month as a wrangler.

His work with the remuda generated high praise from the boss man. The herd of 1,400 or so head gradually made their way from Waco up to Montague County per planned schedule. Early one evening the herd had bedded down for the night. They were only a full day's ride south of the Red River. An abrupt change in the wind brought with it some thunder and lightning along with a brief, but light shower of cold rain. The storm passed quickly and the cattle remained quiet.

During the brief storm, Tadi remained with the horses inside the roped area. A young gelding became spooked from flashes of lightning during the brief change in weather. Tadi attempted to calm the frightened cow pony, but with little success. The horse reared on hind legs repeatedly, each time pawing the air with both fore legs. During the incident one of horse's fore legs came crashing down and its hoof slashed across Tadi's head and face. The young wrangler was knocked to the ground unconscious. The supply wagon driver was nearby and happened to see the accident. He rushed to the Indian boy's aide, draped his body across his saddle horn and transported him quickly to the camp's chuck wagon.

Having little knowledge of what he could do for the bleeding wound across Tadi's face and head, the cook first poured a liberal amount of whiskey over it, and after wiping away some mud and debris, poured a liberal amount of baking flour into the wound hoping it would stop the bleeding. After wrapping Tadi's head in a clean cloth, the injured boy was administered a large amount of whiskey and permitted to rest inside the wagon for the remainder of the night.

On the following afternoon the herd had arrived at the river, and Tadi was brought to my office in Spanish Fort. I spent considerable time cleaning and removing the dried blood and flour from the wound but I marveled at the cook's excellent care. The flour had done its job in controlling the bleeding the night before. I closed Tadi's wound and applied a clean dressing. I felt certain the boy would develop a significant scar in the future.

Tadi's outfit planned on leaving the river on their journey north the following day after a rest for the cattle. Before leaving my office, Tadi with obvious reverence and gratitude, gently touched my forehead and cheek twice on each side. Without speaking, he left my office for his return to the outfit. I will never know, but perhaps that was his Comanche way of giving thanks to me. It was a moment I will always remember.

ooooo

The large number of cattle drives passing through the area and across the Red River were largely responsible for the start of new businesses and increased numbers of people coming there to settle. That growth benefited my medical practice so much that after a short time, my cramped office beside the store was inadequate. New office space became a necessity. After purchase of a lot at the edge of town, I had a two-story building constructed for my office and home.

During this time, Liz and I exchanged an occasional letter. She assured me she was doing well and very happy with her boarding house business that was becoming quite successful. I had no reason not to believe her. As I had requested of her, she began sending small payments from time to time with her letters. Each letter indicated she was much obliged for the change brought in her life. Reading this always brought me joy. Nearly a year passed without a letter, then one finally came with shocking news.

Construction of Sedalia's new Baptist church was finally completed and a clergy arrived soon after to minister to the new church. Following his arrival in town, he became a temporary renter in Liz's boarding house. The sobering news for me came when she mentioned that she and the pastor had married a brief time after his arrival in Sedalia. Her letter conveyed new happiness with her marriage. I responded with a note wishing them well. I felt I had a part to play in Liz's new life and that made me feel good. I felt she was truly a good woman and deserved her new happiness.

25

Emanuel Perez was born out of wedlock in Galveston, Texas, in 1862. Graced with a stunning physical appearance, his black mother had become a sought-after prostitute in Galveston while yet in her teens. Her precocity and beauty caused her to appear older than her age, which benefited her for receiving top dollar tricks in a highly rated Galveston bordello.

Emanuel's father came from Monterrey, Mexico. After arriving in Galveston, he became quite successful working for a gulf cargo company. He found even more success, however, seated nightly at the gaming tables. Francisco Perez demanded and paid only for women of the highest caliber for his pleasure and indiscretions. Emanuel was a product from one of those encounters. Francisco refused to have any part in marriage to the young black prostitute, but willfully tendered Emanuel's mother a fair sum of money that might keep her in style at least while carrying his unborn child.

When, as a small boy being locked in a second floor room while his mother entertained her clients in the room next door, were a few of the memories Emanuel had never forgotten. By age ten, the lad was busy on the streets of Galveston shining wealthy men's boots. At fifteen, he left Galveston and made his way to San Antonio where he was hired on as a hand on one of John Blocker's large outfits preparing to drive a massive herd of nearly 8,000 head to Abilene. Emanuel was to serve as a cook's helper and driver for one of the supply wagons.

Barlo Clement, the outfit's experienced cook, was one of John Blocker's longtime employees on several cattle drives. Clement recognized Emanuel's needs and taught the black boy how to cook and other important things about life in general. The outfit had a day of rest along the Trinity River in Fort Worth. On the following day they planned to continue on their way to the Red River crossing. Around noon of that next day, Emanuel received burns on both arms and hand when moving a large caldron of boiling water from the campfire. Clement prepared a poultice of moist flour and lard and wrapped the boy's arms and hand in clean cloths until he could receive medical attention when the herd reached the Red River.

When the Blocker outfit and their huge herd finally arrived two days later along the Red and were successfully bedded for the night, Emanuel arrived at my office for treatment of his burns. When I removed the trail cook's bandage, the seriousness of his burns was quite evident despite my serious lack of experience with treating burns. I was certain Emanuel's would require some time for healing. I also had great concern about infection developing should he return on the trail.

I did note that young Emanuel was a quiet and unassuming boy with intelligence beyond his years. Considering the extent of his injury and the care required, I suggested that he leave the trail and become my houseboy. This would provide me the opportunity for rendering what care I knew to help the healing of his burns. I was impressed with Emanuel. Flashing a big smile, he accepted my offer. From that day forward, we embarked upon a kinship and loyalty that remained for a very long time.

ooooo

It was a typical warm July summer night in 1882—also my birthday. Quite by chance on that evening an unexpected event took place that would forever change my life. Since my graduation from Penn seventeen years before, I always remained thankful for the rewarding life medicine had given me. My greatest happiness came following that memorable evening inside our town's Masonic Lodge building.

My presence at the Lodge that night was fortuitous for several reasons. I had found that blistering hot and humid July day both busy and tiring. After seeing patients at the office in the early morning hours, I had an uncomfortable trip for a home call some distance down toward Saint Jo. After delivering the Mitchell baby, I finally headed home with plans for spending a quiet and relaxing evening playing cards with Emanuel. I rarely could beat him, but I always enjoyed trying.

I had been well informed that a number of the local women folks were having a bake sale at the Lodge that day. It had been mentioned in our newspaper, and one of my patients had urged me to attend since she was certain I just might find some baked goods to my liking. With some reluctance but out of courtesy to the women folks, I made mind to appear but only for a very brief visit. I had also informed Emanuel that I would be home in a short while for our card game. While at the Lodge that evening I found not only one item very much to my liking, but two!

My penchant for any and all kinds of berry pies sent my tired eyes in search for the right one. I quickly found one that gave me great appeal. While paying one of the ladies for my berry pie and preparing to leave, a very engaging and attractive woman approached. I had never before made her acquaintance.

With a soft pleasant voice she made comment, "I beg your pardon, Dr. Watson. I took notice that you selected my offering for the sale. I and the other ladies do appreciate your purchase. I don't believe we have met. My name is Betsy Anderson. I've heard through Mr. Justin, for whom I work, that you are a fine doctor. I trust you know him?"

Her charm and beguiling physical appearance caught me off guard. I was somewhat chagrined, and it took a moment or two before I could find the right words for a reply. During her introduction, I recognized sincerity and a gentle kindness in her large brown eyes.

Somewhat awkwardly and after collecting my thoughts, I replied, "It gives me great pleasure to make your acquaintance, ma'am. Berry pies are my favorite as you can see, and your pie had every sign of being one of the best. It was too inviting for me to pass up."

Betsy appeared several years my junior. After stepping outside into the night air, we engaged in a friendly and rather lengthy conversation. Her striking personality was compelling and brought me to the point where my fatigue was beginning to fade. My card game with Emanuel would have to wait.

ooooo

After that special night, Betsy and I began to share more time together. I found her personality and charm most pleasing. Early in our relationship she introduced me to her son, Timothy who I found very engaging and a handsome young boy. I could see that Tim had acquired many of his mother's features and mannerisms.

One evening soon after our meeting, I had asked Betsy if she might tell me more about her life and family. She seemed pleased that I showed interest and that I had asked. While sharing coffee in her small house that day, she began her story.

Her family had been farmers in Virginia before moving to Texas. Her father homesteaded property east of Gainesville that bordered the Red River in Cooke County. At the time, her two oldest brothers were quite young. She was born shortly after they arrived in Texas. The Kauffman clan had come from good stock. All were religious and industrious.

With much hard work her parents were successful with their new beginning in Texas. While a young girl living on the farm, Betsy was unhappy and wanted to attend school. A small school had started in Gainesville about that time. She finally persuaded her strict parents to allow her to attend the school during the week and then return home at week's end. This became possible only through the kindness and generosity of Mrs. Carson, a member of the family's church. She had become a war widow and owned a very nice home in Gainesville. She permitted Betsy to live in her home during the week while attending school.

Betsy loved school a great deal and the arrangement she had with Mrs. Carson worked well for them both. She cleaned Mrs. Carson's house in payment for her meals and lodging. When sixteen, Betsy attended a barn dance with a friend one night in Gainesville. That night she was asked to dance by a handsome gentleman several years her senior. His name was Franklin Anderson.

Franklin had grown up in Rhode Island and had served in his state's rifle company in the Union army. After the war and without family ties, his longing for new adventure eventually brought him to Texas. In 1869 Frank began work as a federal brand inspector for cattle herds moving up the Chisholm Trail.

At this point in her story, I could tell she was beginning to tear up. I urged her to continue.

She admitted that she was smitten by the man from Rhode Island that night. Following a brief courtship, she and Franklin were married in Gainesville. In 1871, their son, Tim was born.

Frank continued working as an inspector and their small family prospered. Tragedy struck just after Tim's seventh birthday. Frank was accidentally trampled by a longhorn steer and died a short time after. Betsy became emotionally devastated with her loss. She and Tim remained in Gainesville where sometime later she met a young shoe and boot repairman named Justin. She said that she and Joe Justin became friends, and he was responsible for her being hired in a small shop where he worked.

Betsy then told more about her relationship with Mr. Justin. H.J. Justin, better known as "Joe", had moved to Texas from his home in Indiana and, like everyone else, was filled with adventure. Joe arrived in Gainesville in 1877, if I remember right. He found work repairing boots and shoes in the Norton Shoe Shop. It was there where he set his mind on learning as much as possible about his craft. Betsy joined him working in the Norton shop.

For a period of time, Joe had been watching the growing activity with the trail drives crossing the Red River. He was certain business was there to be had. By that time, his desire was to have his own business making and repairing boots. That enthusiasm and desire led him to Spanish Fort in 1879. With little money he opened a small one-room shop.

Mr. Justin's business grew as he had hoped. The quality of his custom handmade boots brought him a reputation with cowmen far and wide. Before long he was producing two pairs of boots each week. He found that a larger workplace and additional help was needed. In 1881 he requested for Tim and Betsy to leave Gainesville and move to Spanish Fort so that she might assist him in his growing business. Tim was ten years old when they moved.

I was moved by Betsy's story. I, in turn, related much of my life story. Following that night of sharing the happiness and sorrows of our respective lives, we grew closer each day that followed.

26

A year after our meeting at the Lodge, Betsy Anderson and I were married in the small Baptist Church in Spanish Fort. I shared with her the happiest day of my life. Betsy was ten years my junior while Tim was an inquisitive and energetic young boy of eleven.

From that June day, my life had changed and was finally complete. I had a beautiful loving wife and mother for our son whom I treasured. Tim found favor in me, and I in him. Emanuel remained on as our houseboy and became best of friends with Tim.

Betsy continued working with Mr. Justin for a short time following our marriage. On occasion she would assist me in the office. She was never amiss in extending her kindness and gentleness to each of my patients. While sharing time together, Tim began showing me his developing interest in medicine. He accompanied me on frequent occasions when I made country visits, always asking to drive my buggy-hitch. He was full of questions and we grew very close in a short period of time.

Over the years, I had continued exchanging letters with my mother. Even while entering the closing months and years of her life, she had never changed. She always kept me informed about the neighborhood back in Philadelphia and never ceased to fret about her "baby" doctoring those "terrible and dangerous cowboys out west." Mother was delighted when learning of my marriage and the happiness and love I had come to share with Betsy and Tim.

The stubborn and ill-tempered judge, also in failing health, never changed to any degree as the years passed by. Mother did say that age perhaps had brought a slight improvement in his disposition. With my aging parents in failing health, I planned to take Betsy and Tim with me back home. Tim was especially excited to visit Philadelphia and see where I had attended medical school.

We had a very enjoyable trip back east on the train shortly before Father passed away. Seeing my father lying in bed near death was quite emotional for me. For the first time in my life, I saw and accepted the man simply for what he was and had been. I forgave him for the unhappiness he had brought over the years. Of special interest, was my seeing the frail judge's eyes light up when meeting Tim. My father put his pale weak hand on Tim's arm saying in faltered speech, "You look like you'd make a good lawyer, my son!"

Before returning to Texas, Tim and I visited the Penn campus, and in particular the medical school. As always, my boy was filled with questions about Penn and my experiences while there. My mother loved Betsy and Tim. She made a point to tell Betsy stories about her son growing up in Philadelphia.

27

Having now entered the twilight years of my own life, I have found it difficult to believe how many years it had been while I cared for the ills of my patients. I can still recall my student days and then my graduation day at Penn. My return visit there with Betsy and Tim brought back so many memories. And to think on that glorious day how little I knew and understood about people and their frailties of life. I've enjoyed my labors as a doctor, but with the sun now setting on my life, I look forward to my last days with Betsy at my side.

Today, I have only fond memories of the turbulent and thunderous days in Columbia, Sedalia, and then my practice in north Texas along the Red River. Men with differing interests in life, cattle by the millions, and guns blazing away on various occasions all played a part in the thunder that helped mold so many of my experiences and memories.

After the close of the Chisholm, the surrounding area melted into a venue of perpetual
tranquility. Nevertheless, for a young man from
Philadelphia, I believe I adjusted well on the frontier with all its challenges. I have never regretted
leaving Philadelphia and coming west.

The decade of the 1880s in north Texas along
the banks of the Red River was a period of great
transition. The invention and popular use of barbed
wire played a major roll in changing Texas and its
frontier forever. The wide-open range had disappeared. That wire also had a significant bearing
on the closure of the Chisholm Trail after nearly
twenty years of activity.

When a violent tornado roared through northern Montague County one day in the late 1880s,
Red River Station was virtually destroyed. That
horrific storm likely brought with it the greatest thunder heard in the area. Following the violent storm, few buildings remained and the few
remaining survivors had little money or could they
find any good reason for rebuilding the town. The
community had served its purpose at a time when
it was needed most on the Chisholm Trail and in
the county. Gradually, more and more people left
the area for a new beginning elsewhere.

At that time, Betsy and I also made our plans to leave Spanish Fort. By then, Tim was completing four exciting years of medical school at Penn. Like my father and me, graduation day for Tim would bring him honors. Betsy and I traveled to Philadelphia for the special joys that day would bring him—and for me and his mother as well. Our hope was for him to return to Texas for his practice.

In 1887 the Gainesville-Henrietta-Western Railway made its decision to direct its new line south through the town of Nocona. That decision eliminated any future importance for the Spanish Fort community. With closure of the post office that same year, the town nearly ceased to exist.

After the purchase of a small parcel of land and having a home constructed in southern Clay County in 1887, Betsy and I left Spanish Fort. It was also at that time when I chose to end my medical career and begin enjoying my final years with my loving wife.

Not long after our leaving, Mr. Justin's Boot Company and the J. B. March Hardware moved their businesses to Nocona to begin anew. Residents continued to leave Spanish Fort and move to other communities further south in the county.

Following his graduation from Penn after a greatly improved four-year curriculum of study, Tim returned to Texas and chose Fort Worth for his practice. I only wish it had been possible for him to have met and come to know my Uncle Silas. I know my uncle would have been as proud of Tim as I am.

ooooo

Naturally, I have many fond memories of my work with Uncle Silas and the experiences we shared in Columbia and Sedalia. Since coming to Texas, I have met many interesting people along with having many new experiences. I will always remember a number of my patients over the years for their particular maladies and for others with unforgettable personalities. I have special memory of a very young drover I cared for while in Spanish Fort that will forever raise my curiosity.

It occurred one day shortly before the trail closed through River Station. As I recall, I was lost in thought and half asleep sitting alone in my office and enjoying the warm sun coming through my office window. Suddenly, my door burst open. A trail boss, who I had previously come to know, appeared with his injured drover at side. I saw a young sandy-haired boy, barely in his teens. I found a rather severe wound present on his forearm beneath the torn and bloody sleeve of his blouse. I suspected he might have been hooked by a steer's horn.

I could see the boy was likely more nervous and apprehensive about his being in my office than for the wound on his arm. He remained silent yet very cooperative while I cleaned and closed it with thread. I had barely finished applying a dressing on his arm when he suddenly jumped from the table and bolted out my door. I was chagrined since I had not had an opportunity to learn his name. I believed his unexpected exit was simply due to his fear of being in a doctor's office.

The trail boss shared my surprise for the boy's actions and explained that he too was not familiar with the very young drover's name. The boss went on to explain that the boy was a new hired hand and had come to Texas from someplace up in Missouri. He did recall that he'd heard one of the other drovers call the boy Somers—or something like that.

BIBLIOGRAPHY

Abbott, E. C. and H. H. Smith. *We Pointed Them North*. University of Oklahoma Press, 1939.

Addington, Louise. *The Story of Montague County, Its Past and Present*, 1989.

"Agriculture History Series." University of Missouri, Lyndonirwin.com.

Archives and Record Center. "Class of 1865 College of Medicine," University of Pennsylvania, web.

Bartels, Carolyn M. *The Civil War in Missouri—Day By Day—1861–1865*. Burnt District Press, 1992.

Cation, Bruce. *The Civil War*. American Heritage/ Wings Books, 1960.

Cunningham, H.H. *Doctors in Gray*. 2nd ed. 1960, paper ed. 1993, Louisiana State University Press.

Davis, William C. *Brothers in Arms*. New Jersey: Chartwell Books, Edison, 2000.

Davis, William C. *Fighting Men of the Civil War*. New York: Gallery Books, 1989.

Dawson, Treva Tindall and Gayle Cochran-Smith. *Memories along the Chisholm Trail*, 2012.

Forney, Mathias N. *Car Builder's Dictionary*, Internet Archive.

Genealogy Trails, "History of Cattle Drives," cattle drives.com.

"History Laid to Rest" *Higginsville* 114, no. 85 (1992).

Hunter, J. Marvin, *The Trail Drivers of Texas*. Texas: University of Texas Press, 1924.

Imhauser, Becky Carr. *All Along Ohio Street, Sedalia, Missouri*. 2nd ed. Missouri: Wallsworth Publishing.

Missouri Department of Natural Resources Museum. "A State Divided – Missouri and the Civil War," dhr.mo.gov./

Missouri Department of Natural Resources. "Battle of Lexington – September 18–20, 1861." State Historical Site, Lexington, Missouri, dhr.mo.gov.

McGaugh, Scott. *Surgeon in Blue*. New York: Arcade Publishing, 2013.

Mudd, Joseph A. *With Porter in North Missouri.* 1992 reprint: Iowa Press of the Camp Pope Bookshop.

Porter, W. R. *History of Montague County, Texas,* 1995.

Richley, Myrna. "Family Records—Kansas–Missouri Border Wars."

Richley, Myrna. "Family Records—The Younger Brothers."

Richley, Myrna. "Family Records—The James Boys, Frank and Jesse."

Richley, Myrna. "Personal Family Genealogy Records," 2013.

Round Up Magazine, Western Writers of America. "A Tribute to Frontier Doctors," August 2002.

Secretary, State of Texas. "Digital Heritage," sos. state .tx.us

Settles, Thomas M. *John Bankhead Magruder.* Louisiana State University Press, 2009.

State of Missouri, Official Manual. "The Roll of the Negro in Missouri History, 1973–74," sos. mo.gov.

State of Texas Historical Records. "History of Spanish Fort, Texas," 1988, web.

State of Texas Historical Society. "Handbook of Texas," web.

Steele, Philip W. *Starr Treks—Belle and Pearl Starr*. Louisiana Pelican Publishing, 1998.

Stephens, Larry. *John Gatewood, Confederate Bushwacker*. Louisiana Pelican Publishing, 2012.

Strickland, Rennard. *The Indians of Oklahoma*. University of Oklahoma Press, 1980.

Sweeney, Thomas. "Civil War Era Medicine," web.

Theis, Randall M. "What Would His Skull Be Worth? Quantrill's Posthumous Sojourn in Kansas." *Kansas Heritage*. August, 1993.

US Department of Interior, "National Registry of Historic Places," doi.gov.

Welton, Will. "Frontier Doctors in Indian Territory, Oklahoma," weltonusa.com

Wolk, Gregory. *A Tour Guide to Missouri's Civil War*. Missouri Monogram Publishing, 2010.